Agatha Christie

4.50 From Paddington

Collins

Collins

HarperCollins Publishers
The News Building
1 London Bridge Street
London SE1 9GF

www.collinselt.com

Collins® is a registered trademark of HarperCollins Publishers Limited.

This *Collins English Readers* edition first published by HarperCollins
Publishers 2012. This second edition published 2017.

10 9 8 7 6 5 4 3 2 1

First published in Great Britain by Collins 1957

www.agathachristie.com

ISBN: 978-0-00-826239-6

A catalogue record for this book is available from the British Library.

Cover design © HarperCollins*Publishers* Ltd/Agatha Christie Ltd 2017

Typeset by Davidson Publishing Solutions, Glasgow

Printed and bound by CPI Group (UK) Ltd., Croydon, CR0 4YY

Contents

♦ INTRODUCTION ♦

ABOUT COLLINS ENGLISH READERS

Collins English Readers have been created for readers worldwide whose first language is not English. The stories are carefully graded to ensure that you, the reader, will both enjoy and benefit from your reading experience.

Words which are above the required reading level are underlined the first time they appear in a story. All underlined words are defined in the **Glossary** at the back of the book. Books at levels 1 and 2 take their definitions from the *Collins COBUILD Essential English Dictionary*, and books at levels 3 and above from the *Collins COBUILD Advanced English Dictionary*. Where appropriate, definitions are simplified for level and context.

Alongside the glossary, a **Character list** is provided to help the reader identify who is who, and how they are connected to each other. **Cultural notes** explain historical, cultural and other references. **Maps and diagrams** are provided where appropriate. A **downloadable recording** is also available of the full story. To access the audio, go to www.collinselt.com/eltreadersaudio. The password is the second word on page 2 of this book.

To support both teachers and learners, additional materials are available online at www.collinselt.com/readers. These include a **Plot synopsis** and **classroom activities** (both for teachers), **Student activities**, a **level checker** and much more.

ABOUT AGATHA CHRISTIE

Agatha Christie (1890–1976) is known throughout the world as the Queen of Crime. She is the most widely published and translated author of all time and in any language; only the Bible and Shakespeare have sold more copies.

Agatha Christie's first novel was published in 1920. It featured Hercule Poirot, the Belgian detective who has become the most popular detective in crime fiction since Sherlock Holmes.

Collins has published Agatha Christie since 1926.

THE GRADING SCHEME

The Collins COBUILD Grading Scheme has been created using the most up-to-date language usage information available today. Each level is guided by a comprehensive grammar and vocabulary framework, ensuring that the series will perfectly match readers' abilities.

		CEF band	Pages	Word count	Headwords
Level 1	elementary	A2	64	5,000–8,000	approx. 700
Level 2	pre-intermediate	A2–B1	80	8,000–11,000	approx. 900
Level 3	intermediate	B1	96	11,000–20,000	approx. 1,300
Level 4	upper-intermediate	B2	112-128	15,000–26,000	approx. 1,700
Level 5	upper-intermediate+	B2+	128+	22,000–30,000	approx. 2,200
Level 6	advanced	C1	144+	28,000+	2,500+
Level 7	advanced+	C2	160+	*varied*	*varied*

For more information on the Collins COBUILD Grading Scheme go to www.collinselt.com/readers/gradingscheme.

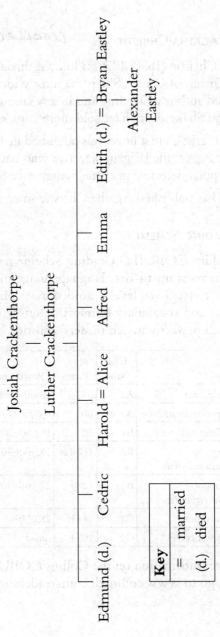

Crackenthorpe Family Tree

Josiah Crackenthorpe

Luther Crackenthorpe

Edmund (d.)　Cedric　Harold = Alice　Alfred　Emma　Edith (d.) = Bryan Eastley

Alexander
Eastley

Key	
=	married
(d.)	died

Chapter 1

Mrs Elspeth McGillicuddy hurried along Platform 3 at Paddington Station[1] after the <u>porter</u> who was carrying her suitcase. Mrs McGillicuddy was short and the porter was tall. Mrs McGillicuddy was also carrying a lot of packages after a day of Christmas shopping. So the porter had already turned the corner at the end of the platform while she searched her bag for the ticket at the entrance gate.

At that moment, a voice sounded above her head, 'The train standing at Platform 3, is the 4.50 for Brackhampton, Milchester, Waverton, Roxeter and stations to Chadmouth. Passengers for Brackhampton and Milchester travel at the back of the train.'

Mrs McGillicuddy found her ticket and showed it to the man at the gate who said, 'On the right, at the back.'

Mrs McGillicuddy continued up the platform and found her porter waiting outside the door of a third-<u>class</u>[2] carriage.

'I'm travelling first-class,' said Mrs McGillicuddy.

'You didn't say so,' said the porter. Mrs McGillicuddy, *had* said so, but was too tired to argue.

The porter carried her suitcase to the next <u>coach</u>, where Mrs McGillicuddy sat down alone and opened her magazine. Five minutes later, whistles blew, and the train started. The magazine slipped from Mrs McGillicuddy's hand, her head dropped sideways and three minutes later she was asleep. She slept for thirty-five minutes and awoke feeling much better as she sat looking out of the window at the countryside flying past. It was almost dark now and the train passed through a station, then began to slow down, and then it stopped for a short while before it began to move forward again.

A train passed them, going in the opposite direction. Then another train, going in the same direction, passed frighteningly close to them. For a time the two trains ran <u>parallel</u>, and Mrs McGillicuddy looked from her window into the windows of the other carriages. Most of the <u>blinds</u> were down, but occasionally she could see people in the carriages, although many of them were empty.

Suddenly, when the two trains seemed to have stopped because they were both moving at the same slow speed, a blind flew up and Mrs McGillicuddy looked into the lighted first-class carriage that was only a short distance away.

Then she <u>gasped</u> and stood up.

Standing with his back to the window was a man. His hands were round the throat of a woman, and he was slowly <u>strangling</u> her. Her eyes were wide open and her face was purple. As Mrs McGillicuddy watched, the woman's body collapsed. At the same time, the other train began to go forward faster and a moment later it had passed Mrs McGillicuddy's train and disappeared.

Then the door of her carriage opened and a man said, 'Ticket, please.'

Mrs McGillicuddy turned to him, 'A woman has been strangled in a train that has just passed ours. I saw it – through there.' She pointed to the window. 'You must *do* something at once!'

The ticket collector[2] coughed. 'You don't think that you may have been asleep and – er—?'

'I have been asleep, but if you think this was a dream, you're wrong. I *saw* it, I tell you.'

The ticket collector looked at his watch. 'We shall be in Brackhampton in seven minutes. I will report what you have told me. Perhaps you could give me your name and address…'

Mrs McGillicuddy gave him the address where she would be staying for the next few days and her home address in Scotland.

The train was slowing down now, and running through the bright lights of a large town. As it moved towards a crowded platform, the usual voice was saying, 'The train now arriving at Platform 1 is the 5.38 for Milchester, Waverton, Roxeter, and stations to Chadmouth...'

Her mind went back to the scene on the other train. Awful, really awful... and if the blind of the carriage had not by chance flown up... then she would not have been a witness to the crime.

Voices shouted, whistles blew, doors were banged shut. The 5.38 moved slowly out of Brackhampton station. An hour and five minutes later it stopped at Milchester. Mrs McGillicuddy collected her packages and her suitcase and got out.

Outside the station, a taxi driver came forward, 'Are you Mrs McGillicuddy? For St Mary Mead?'

It was a nine-mile drive, but at last the taxi reached the familiar village street and finally stopped. Mrs McGillicuddy got out and walked up the brick path to the door, which was opened by a servant. While the driver put her bags inside, Mrs McGillicuddy walked straight through the hall to where, at the open sitting room door, stood a <u>fragile</u> old lady.

'Elspeth!'

'Jane!'

They kissed and then, without a pause, Mrs McGillicuddy cried, 'Oh, Jane, I've just seen a *murder*!'

CHAPTER 2

Miss Marple did not look surprised as she said, 'Most upsetting for you, Elspeth. I think you should tell me about it at once.'

That was exactly what Mrs McGillicuddy wanted to do. So she sat down by the fire and told her story while Miss Marple listened.

When she had finished, Miss Marple spoke, 'The best thing, I think, is for you to go upstairs and have a wash. Then we will have dinner – during which we will not discuss this at all. After dinner we can discuss it from every point of view.'

So the two ladies had dinner, discussing life in St Mary Mead, and also their gardens. Then they settled themselves by the fire again, and Miss Marple took out two beautiful old glasses from a corner cupboard, and from another cupboard took out a bottle.

'No coffee tonight for you, Elspeth. You are already over-excited (and no wonder!) so I suggest you have a glass of my home-made wine.'

'Jane,' said Mrs McGillicuddy, as she took an enjoyable <u>sip</u>, 'you don't think, do you, that I imagined it?'

'Certainly not,' said Miss Marple.

'<u>Thank goodness</u>. Because that ticket collector, *he* thought so. Very polite, but...'

'I think, Elspeth, that he behaved quite normally. It sounds – and indeed is – a very strange story. But I do not doubt at all that you saw what you've told me you saw. The man had his back to you, so you didn't see his face?'

'No.'

'And the woman, can you describe her? Young, old?'

'Between thirty and thirty-five, I think.'

'Good-looking?'

'I don't know. Her face, you see, was all...'

4

Miss Marple said quickly, 'Yes, yes, I understand. How was she dressed?'

'She had on a pale-coloured fur coat. No hat. Her hair was blonde.'

'And there was nothing particular that you can remember about the man?'

Mrs McGillicuddy took a little time to think before she replied. 'He was tall – and dark-haired, I think. He had a heavy coat on.'

Miss Marple paused. 'We shall know more, I expect, in the morning.'

'In the morning?'

'Well, it will be in the morning newspapers. After this man had killed her, he would be left with a body. So he would probably leave the train at the next station – can you remember if the carriage had a corridor²?'

'No, it did not.'

'Then it was a train that was not going far, so it would stop at Brackhampton. He left the train at Brackhampton, perhaps, after arranging the body in a corner seat. But of course she will soon be discovered – and the news will almost certainly be in the morning papers.'

II

But it was not in the morning papers.

Miss Marple and Mrs McGillicuddy, after making sure of this, finished their breakfast in silence. Then Mrs McGillicuddy stood up and turned to her friend.

'Well?'

'I think,' said Miss Marple, 'we should walk down to the police station and talk to Sergeant Cornish. I know him very well so I think he'll listen – and pass the information on to the right department.'

Frank Cornish was friendly and polite. He listened to Mrs McGillicuddy's story and after she had finished he said, 'That sounds very strange.'

But Miss Marple believed that her friend was telling the truth, and he knew all about Miss Marple. She looked soft and fragile, but really she was as sharp and as clever as it was possible to be.

He said, 'Of course, you may have made a mistake – I'm not saying you did – but a lot of joking goes on – it might not have been serious and the woman might not have been dead.'

'I know what I saw,' said Mrs McGillicuddy.

Cornish said, 'You have done everything correctly and you can trust me to start inquiries.' He turned to Miss Marple. 'What do you think has happened to the body?'

'There seem to be only two possibilities,' said Miss Marple. 'The most likely one was that the body was left in the train, but that seems unlikely now, for it would have been found last night. The only other thing the murderer could have done would be to push the body out of the train onto the track. So it must be on the track somewhere – though that also seems unlikely.'

'Yes,' said Cornish. 'The body, if there is a body, ought to have been discovered by now, or will be very soon.'

But that day passed and the next day. On that evening Miss Marple received a note from Sergeant Cornish.

Considering the matter about which you spoke to me, full inquiries have been made, with no result. No woman's body has been found. I suggest that your friend may have witnessed a scene just as she described, but that it was much less serious than she thought.

CHAPTER 3

'Less serious? Nonsense!' said Mrs McGillicuddy. 'It was murder!' She looked at Miss Marple and Miss Marple looked back at her. 'Go on, Jane, say I imagined the whole thing! That's what you think now, isn't it?'

'Anyone *can* be mistaken,' Miss Marple said gently, 'although I think that you were probably *not* mistaken… But I don't think there's anything more you can do.'

'That's a relief, in a way,' said Mrs McGillicuddy, 'as I'm going out to Ceylon after Christmas to stay with my son Roderick, and I do not want to put off that visit. So if the police choose to be stupid—'

Miss Marple shook her head. 'Oh, no, the police aren't stupid. And that makes it interesting, doesn't it?'

Mrs McGillicuddy looked surprised.

'One wants to know,' said Miss Marple, 'who killed the woman, and why, and what happened to her body.'

'That's for the police to find out.'

'Exactly – and they haven't found out. Which means that the man was very clever. I can't imagine how he got rid of it. You kill a woman in sudden anger – it can't have been planned, you would never choose to kill someone just before arriving at a big station. So you strangle her – and then what can you do…?' Miss Marple paused.

Mrs McGillicuddy said, 'Well, I am going to stop thinking about it and start thinking about the trains to London tomorrow. Would the afternoon be all right? I'm going to my daughter Margaret's for tea.'

'I wonder, Elspeth, if you would mind taking the 12.15? We could have an early lunch. And I wonder, too, if Margaret would mind if you didn't arrive for tea – if you arrived about seven, perhaps?'

Mrs McGillicuddy looked at her friend with interest. 'Are you planning something, Jane?'

'I suggest, Elspeth, that I could travel up to London with you, and that we could then travel back to Brackhampton in a train at the same time as you travelled the other day. You could then return to London and I would come on here as you did. *I*, of course, would pay the fares,' Miss Marple said clearly.

'What do you expect, Jane? Another murder?'

'Certainly not. But I would like to see for myself exactly where the crime was committed.'

And so the next day Miss Marple and Mrs McGillicuddy sat in two opposite corners of a first-class carriage speeding out of London on the 4.50 from Paddington. But on this occasion no train passed close to them going in the same direction. A few trains flashed past them towards London. On two occasions trains flashed past them going the other way.

'We're due in Brackhampton in five minutes,' said Miss Marple.

A ticket collector appeared at the door. Miss Marple looked at Mrs McGillicuddy, who shook her head. It was not the same ticket collector. He looked at their tickets, and moved on a little unsteadily as the train swung round a long curve slowing down as it did so. There were lights flashing past outside, buildings, and they could see a few streets and buses.

'We'll be there in a minute,' said Mrs McGillicuddy, 'and I can't really see this journey has been any good *at all*.'

'But this train is a few minutes late. Was yours on time on Friday?'

'I think so.'

The train ran slowly into Brackhampton station. Doors opened and shut, people got in and out. Easy, thought Miss Marple, for a murderer to leave the station amongst all those people, or even to find another carriage and go on in the train to the end of its journey. But not so easy to make a body disappear into the air. That body must be *somewhere*.

Mrs McGillicuddy had got out and spoke now through the open window. 'Take care of yourself, Jane. And don't let's worry ourselves any more about all this. We've done what we could.'

Miss Marple nodded. 'Goodbye, Elspeth. A happy Christmas to you.'

A whistle blew and the train began to move, but Miss Marple did not lean back as it increased speed. Instead she sat upright. Mrs McGillicuddy had said that they had both done all that they could do. It was true of Mrs McGillicuddy, but about herself Miss Marple did not feel so sure.

Like a <u>General</u> planning a possible battle, Miss Marple thought through the facts for and against further action. For further action were the following:

1. *My long experience of life and human nature.*
2. *Sir Henry Clithering and his <u>godson</u> (now at <u>Scotland Yard</u>), who was so very nice in the Little Paddocks case.*
3. *My nephew Raymond's second boy, David, who works for British Railways.*
4. *Griselda's boy, Leonard, who knows so much about maps.*

'But I can't go here, there and everywhere, making inquiries and finding out things. I'm too old for any more adventures,' she thought, watching out of the window the curving line of an <u>embankment</u>[3]...

A curve...

Very faintly something came into her mind… Just after the ticket collector had seen their tickets… It suggested an idea. A completely different idea…

Suddenly Miss Marple did not feel old at all!

II

The next morning Miss Marple wrote to her nephew's son, David West, asking for important information.

Fortunately she was invited, as usual, to Griselda's house for Christmas dinner, and here she was able to ask young Leonard about maps.

Leonard loved maps of all kinds and did not wonder why Miss Marple was interested in a <u>large-scale</u> map of a particular area. He even found one amongst his collection and lent it to her.

III

Soon Miss Marple received a letter from David West. It said:

Dear Aunt Jane,

I've got the information you wanted. There is only one train that it can be – the 4.33, which is a slow train and stops at Haling Broadway, Barwell Heath, Brackhampton and then stations to Market Basing.

So, do I smell some village scandal? Did you, returning from Christmas shopping in London by the 4.50, see the <u>vicar's</u> wife being kissed by the Tax Inspector? But why does it matter which train it was?

Yours ever,
David

Miss Marple smiled. It seemed that some more travelling was necessary.

She went up to London as before on the 12.15, but this time returned not by the 4.50, but by the 4.33 in an empty first-class carriage. As the train came near to Brackhampton, running around a curve, Miss Marple pulled down the blind and then stood with her back to the window.

Yes, she decided, the sudden curving of the line did throw one back against the window and the blind might very easily fly up. She looked out of the window. It was only just dark, but to see things clearly she must make a daylight journey.

The next day she went up to London by the early morning train. Then a quarter of an hour before she reached Brackhampton, Miss Marple got out the map which Leonard had lent her. She could see exactly where she was just as the train began to slow down for a curve. It was a very big curve and Miss Marple divided her attention between watching the ground beneath her and looking at the map until the train finally ran into Brackhampton.

That night she wrote a letter to Miss Florence Hill, at 4 Madison Road, Brackhampton. And the next morning she went to the library to read about the local history of the area. Her idea of what had happened was possible but there was nothing to prove it yet. And that would need action, the kind of action she was not strong enough to take. If her theory were to be definitely proved or not, she must have help. The question was – who? Miss Marple thought for a long time. Then suddenly she smiled and said aloud a name.

'Of course! Lucy Eyelesbarrow!'

CHAPTER 4

Lucy Eyelesbarrow was thirty-two. She had taken a <u>First</u> in Mathematics at Oxford, and was expected to have a successful academic life. But Lucy Eyelesbarrow, as well as being very clever, was also very sensible. She knew that <u>scholars</u> were not well-paid, and she liked money. And to make money she knew that one must do work that is highly valued because there are always too few people to do it. So, to the great surprise of her friends and other scholars, Lucy Eyelesbarrow decided to become a highly-skilled professional at housework.

Her success was immediate. Now, after about ten years, she was known all over Britain. It was quite usual for wives to say happily to their husbands, 'It will be all right. I *can* go with you to America. *I've got Lucy Eyelesbarrow!*' Because once she came into a house, all the worry and hard work went out of it. Lucy Eyelesbarrow did everything. She looked after old people and young children, got on well with servants, and was wonderful with dogs. She also cooked perfectly. Best of all she never minded what she did. She washed the kitchen floor, dug the garden, and carried coal!

One of her rules was never to accept any job for a long time: two weeks or four at the most.

Lucy read the letter from Miss Marple. She had met her two years ago when Raymond West, the novelist, had paid for her to look after his old aunt who had been ill. Lucy had liked Miss Marple very much and now the old lady was asking if she could do a certain job for her – rather an *unusual* one. Perhaps Miss Eyelesbarrow could meet her so they could discuss it.

So the next day they met alone in a small, dark writing room of Lucy Eyelesbarrow's club in London. She said, 'I'm rather busy at the moment, but perhaps you can tell me what it is you want me to do?'

'It's very simple, really,' said Miss Marple. 'Unusual, but simple. I want you to find a body.'

'What kind of a body?' asked Lucy Eyelesbarrow calmly.

'The body of a woman,' said Miss Marple, 'who was strangled in a train.'

'Well, that's certainly unusual. Tell me about it.'

Miss Marple told her. Lucy Eyelesbarrow listened without interrupting. At the end she said, 'Well, what do you want me to do?'

'I've got a theory,' said Miss Marple. 'The body's got to be *somewhere*. If it wasn't found in the train, then it must have been pushed out of the train – but it hasn't been found anywhere on the line. So I travelled down the same way to see if there was a place where the body could have been thrown off the train and yet not on to the line – and there was. The railway line makes a big curve before getting into Brackhampton, on the edge of a high embankment. If a body was thrown out there, when the train was leaning to one side, I *think* it would fall right down the embankment.'

'But surely it would still be found – even there?'

'Oh, yes. It would have to be taken away… Here's the place – on this map.'

Lucy studied the place where Miss Marple's finger pointed.

'It is right on the edge of Brackhampton now,' said Miss Marple, 'but it used to be a country house with large grounds and it's still there – surrounded by <u>housing estates</u>. It's called Rutherford Hall. It was built by a man called Crackenthorpe, a very rich manufacturer, in 1884. The original Crackenthorpe's son, an elderly man, is living there still with, I hear, a daughter. The railway surrounds half of the property.'

'And you want me to do – what?'

'I want you to get a job there. But it might, you know, be *dangerous.*'

'I don't know,' said Lucy 'I don't think danger would worry me.'

'I didn't think it would,' said Miss Marple.

'What do I look for exactly?'

'Any signs along the embankment, a piece of clothing, broken bushes – that kind of thing.'

'And then?' Lucy asked.

'I shall be staying nearby,' said Miss Marple. 'With an old servant of mine, Florence, who lives in Brackhampton. I think you should mention you have an aunt living in the neighbourhood and that you want a job that is close to her, and also that you need some spare time so that you can go and see her.'

'I was going on holiday the day after tomorrow,' Lucy said. 'That can wait. But I can only stay three weeks. After that, I have another job.'

'If we can't find out anything in three weeks, we might as well give up the whole thing,' said Miss Marple.

After Miss Marple had gone, Lucy rang up an Employment Office in Brackhampton, and explained she needed a job in the neighbourhood to be near her 'aunt'. After saying no to several more desirable places, Rutherford Hall was mentioned.

'That sounds exactly what I want,' said Lucy.

II

Two days later, driving her own small car, Lucy Eyelesbarrow passed between two large iron gates. A long <u>drive</u> wound between dark bushes up to Rutherford Hall, which was like a small castle. But the stone steps in front of the door were broken and the drive was green with <u>weeds</u>.

She pulled an old bell, and an untidy woman opened the door. 'Miss Eyelesbarrow?'

'That's right,' said Lucy.

The house was very cold inside. The woman led her along a dark hall and opened a door. To Lucy's surprise, it was a rather pleasant sitting room, with books and pretty chairs.

'I'll tell Miss Crackenthorpe you're here,' said the woman, and went away shutting the door.

After a few minutes the door opened again. Emma Crackenthorpe was a middle-aged woman, neither good-looking nor <u>plain</u>, sensibly dressed in warm clothes, with dark hair and light brown eyes.

'Miss Eyelesbarrow?' She held out her hand. Then she looked doubtful. She had clearly been expecting someone very different from Lucy. 'I wonder, if this job is really right for you? I don't want someone just to organize things, I want someone to do the work.'

Lucy said, 'You want cooking and washing-up, and housework. That's what I do.'

'It's a big house, you know, and we only live in part of it – my father and myself. I have several brothers, but they are not here very often. Two women come in, a Mrs Kidder in the morning, and Mrs Hart three days a week.' She paused. 'My father is old and a little – difficult sometimes. I wouldn't like—'

Lucy said quickly, 'I'm very used to old people, and I always manage to get on well with them.'

Emma Crackenthorpe looked pleased. Lucy was given a large dark bedroom with a small electric heater, and was shown round the house. As they passed a door in the hall a voice shouted, 'Is that you, Emma? Have you got the new girl there? Bring her in. I want to look at her.'

The two women entered the room. Old Mr Crackenthorpe was stretched out in a chair. He was a big, but thin man with thick grey hair, a large chin and small, lively eyes. 'Let's have a look at you, young lady.'

Lucy advanced, confident and smiling.

'There's one thing you must understand straight away. Just because we live in a big house doesn't mean we're rich. We're *not* rich[4]. We live simply – do you hear? – *simply!* I live here because my father built the house and I like it.'

'<u>Your home is your castle</u>,' said Lucy.

'You're laughing at me?'

'Of course not. I think it's very exciting to have a real country place all surrounded by a town.'

'Exactly. Fields with cows in them – right in the middle of Brackhampton.'

Lucy and Emma left the room and Lucy asked the times of meals and inspected the kitchen. Then she said cheerfully, 'Just leave everything to me.'

Lucy got up at six the next morning. She cleaned the house, prepared vegetables, cooked and served breakfast. With Mrs Kidder she made the beds and at eleven o'clock they sat down for some tea in the kitchen

Mrs Kidder was a small, thin woman. 'Miss Emma has to put up with a lot from her father,' she said. 'He's so mean. But she's not weak. And when the gentlemen come down she makes sure there's something good to eat.'

'The gentlemen?'

'Yes. It was a big family. The <u>eldest</u>, Mr Edmund, he was killed in the war. Then there's Mr Cedric, he lives abroad somewhere. He paints pictures. Mr Harold works in the City, in London – he married a lord's daughter. Then there's Mr Alfred.'

He seems very nice, but he's been in trouble once or twice – and there's Miss Edith's husband, Mr Bryan, ever so nice, he is – she died some years ago; and there's Master Alexander, their little boy. He's at school, but comes here for the holidays.'[5]

Lucy listened carefully to all this information. When Mrs Kidder had gone, she cooked lunch and when she had cleared it away and washed up, she was ready to start exploring.

First, she walked round the gardens. A flower border near the house was the only place that was free of weeds. The gardener was a very old man, who was only pretending to work in the kitchen garden. Lucy spoke to him pleasantly. He lived in a cottage nearby and behind his cottage was a drive that led through the park, and under a railway <u>arch</u> into a rough path.

Every few minutes a train ran over the arch. Lucy watched the trains as they slowed down to go round the sharp curve surrounding the Crackenthorpe property. She passed under the railway arch and out into the road. On one side was the railway embankment, on the other was a high wall and some factory buildings. Lucy walked along the path until it came out into a street of small houses. A woman was walking past and Lucy stopped her.

'Excuse me, can you tell me if there is a public telephone near here?'

'There's one at the Post Office at the corner of the road.'

Lucy thanked her and walked along until she came to the Post Office. There was a telephone box at one side. She went into it, dialled and asked to speak to Miss Marple.

A woman's voice said, 'She's resting. And I'm not going to wake her! Who shall I say called?'

'Miss Eyelesbarrow. Just tell her that I've arrived and that I'll let her know when I have any news.'

CHAPTER 5

The next day in the sitting room after lunch Lucy said to Emma, 'Will it be all right if I just practise a few golf shots in the park?'

'Oh, yes, certainly. How clever of you to play golf.'

'I'm not much good, but it's a pleasanter form of exercise than just going for a walk.'

'There's nowhere to walk outside this place,' said Mr Crackenthorpe. 'Nothing but pavements and miserable little box houses. They'd like to buy my land and build more of them. But they won't until I'm dead. And I'm not going to die to please anybody. I can tell you *that*! I know what they're waiting for. Cedric, and Harold, and Alfred… I'm surprised he hasn't tried to get rid of me already. And perhaps he did, at Christmas-time. That was a very strange stomach upset I had. Dr Quimper asked me a lot of questions about it.'

'Everyone gets stomach upsets sometimes, Father,' said Emma.

'All right, all right, say that I ate too much! That's what you mean. And *why* did I eat too much? Because there was too much food on the table. And that reminds me – you, young woman, you sent in five potatoes for lunch. Two potatoes are enough for anybody. So don't send in more than four in future. The extra one was wasted today.'[4]

'It wasn't wasted, Mr Crackenthorpe. I am going to use it in a Spanish omelette tonight.'

As Lucy went out of the room she heard him say, 'She's always got an answer! She cooks well, though – and she's a good-looking girl.'

Lucy Eyelesbarrow took a golf club out of the set she had brought with her, and walked out into the park. She hit the ball a few times until it landed on the railway embankment, then went up and began to look about for it. During the afternoon she searched about a third of the embankment. Nothing.

Then, on the next day, she did find something. A rose bush growing on the bank had been broken. Caught on it was a small piece of pale brown fur. Lucy took some scissors out of her pocket and cut it in half. The half she had cut off she put in an envelope.

As she came down the steep slope, she looked carefully at the long grass and at the bottom of the embankment just below the broken rose bush she found a powder compact. She put it in her pocket.

On the following afternoon, Lucy got into her car and went to see her 'aunt'. Number 4 Madison Road was a small, grey house in a small, grey street, but it had a very clean front step. The door was opened by a tall woman dressed in black who took her to Miss Marple, who was in the sitting room by the fire.

'Well!' Lucy said. 'It looks as though you were right.' She showed Miss Marple what she had found and told her how she had found them.

Miss Marple felt the small piece of fur. 'Elspeth said the woman was wearing a light-coloured fur coat. I suppose the compact was in the pocket of the coat and fell out as the body rolled down the slope. You didn't take all the fur?'

'No, I left half of it on the bush.'

'Very good. The police will want to check it.'

'You are going to the police – with these things?'

'Well – not yet… It would be better, I think, to find the body first.'

'But won't that be very difficult? I mean, the murderer may have taken it *anywhere*.'

'Not *anywhere*,' said Miss Marple. 'Because then he might much more easily have killed the girl in some remote place and driven the body away from there. You haven't understood...'

Lucy interrupted. 'Do you mean – that this crime was planned?'

'I didn't think so at first,' said Miss Marple. 'But isn't it hard to believe that a man suddenly killed a woman, then looked out of the window and saw the train going round a curve exactly at a place where he could push the body out, *and* where he could go later and remove it! If he had just thrown her out there by chance, he wouldn't have done anything else and the body would have been found. I think that he *must* have known all about Rutherford Hall, its geographical position, I mean – an island surrounded by railway lines.'

'It is exactly like that,' said Lucy.

'So if the murderer came to Rutherford Hall that night, before anyone could discover the body the next day, how would he come?'

Lucy thought. 'There's a rough path, beside a factory wall. He would probably come that way, turn in under the railway arch and along the back drive. Then he could go to the bottom of the embankment, find the body, and carry it back to the car.'

'And then,' continued Miss Marple, 'he took it to some place he had already chosen near Rutherford Hall. The obvious thing, I suppose, would be to bury it somewhere.'

'It wouldn't be easy,' said Lucy. 'He couldn't bury it in the park, because someone would notice it.'

'Then in some farm building?'

'That would be simpler... There are a lot of old buildings that nobody ever goes near.'

II

So the next afternoon Lucy looked around some of the old farm buildings. Suddenly she heard someone cough and turned to see the gardener, looking at her.

'You should be careful' he said. 'That floor is not safe. And you were up those steps just now and they aren't safe either.'

'I was just wondering if this place could be used for growing things,' Lucy said cheerfully. 'Everything seems to be <u>in ruins</u>.'

'That's because the <u>Master</u> won't spend any money.'

'But the place could make money – if the buildings were mended.'

'He doesn't want to make money. He knows what will happen after he's dead – the young gentlemen will sell the whole place as fast as they can. They're going to get a lot of money when he dies.'

'I suppose he's a very rich man?' said Lucy.

'Crackenthorpe's Delights, that's what the business was called. Mr Crackenthorpe's father started it and made his fortune. His two sons were educated to be gentlemen and they weren't interested in their father's business. The younger one was killed in a car accident. The older one went abroad a lot when he was young, and bought a lot of old statues and had them sent home. They didn't get on well, him and his father.'

'But after his father died, the older Mr Crackenthorpe came and lived here?'

'Him and his family, yes, in 1928.'

Lucy went back to the house and found Emma Crackenthorpe standing in the hall, reading a letter. 'My nephew Alexander will be here tomorrow – with a school friend. Alexander's room is the first one at the top of the stairs. The one next to it will do for his friend, James Stoddart-West,' she said.

'Yes, Miss Crackenthorpe, I'll prepare both rooms.'

'They'll arrive before lunch.' Emma paused. 'I expect they'll be hungry.'

'Roast chicken, do you think?' said Lucy. 'And apple tart?'

'Alexander's very fond of apple tart.'

The two boys arrived the next morning. Alexander Eastley had fair hair and blue eyes, Stoddart-West was dark and wore glasses. During lunch they talked seriously about sport, and occasionally about space travel. The roast chicken was eaten very quickly and every bit of apple tart disappeared.[5]

Mr Crackenthorpe said, 'You two will soon eat all my money.'

Alexander looked at him. 'We'll have bread and cheese if you can't afford meat, Grandfather.'

'Of course I can *afford* it but I don't like waste.'

'We haven't wasted any, sir,' said Stoddart-West, looking down at his empty plate.

After she had washed up, Lucy went out. She could hear the boys calling to each other on the <u>lawn</u>. She went down the front drive and began to hunt amongst the bushes with the help of her golf club. Suddenly the polite voice of Alexander Eastley made her turn.

'Are you looking for something, Miss Eyelesbarrow?'

'A golf ball,' said Lucy. 'Several golf balls in fact.'

'We'll help you,' said Alexander.

'That's very kind of you. I thought you were playing football.'

'One can't go *on* playing football,' explained Stoddart-West. 'One gets too hot. Do you play a lot of golf?'

'I do enjoy it, but I don't get much opportunity.'

'There's a <u>clock golf</u> set in the house,' Alexander said. 'We could fix it up on the lawn and have a game.'

Encouraged by Lucy, the boys went off to get it. Later, as she returned to the house, she found them setting it out on the lawn.

'It's a pity the set is so old,' said Stoddart-West. 'You can hardly see the numbers.'

'It needs some white paint,' said Lucy. 'You could get some tomorrow.'

'Good idea.' Alexander said. 'But I think there are some old pots of paint in the Long <u>Barn</u>. Shall we go and look?'

'What's the Long Barn?' asked Lucy.

Alexander pointed to a long, stone building near the back drive. 'A lot of grandfather's statue collection is in there. And it is sometimes used for Women's Institute events[6]. Come and see it.'

Lucy followed the boys to the barn, which had a big wooden door. Alexander took a a key from a nail near the top of the door, then he turned it in the lock. Inside there were three big, ugly statues, and an even bigger <u>sarcophagus</u>. Besides these, there were two folding tables and some piles of chairs. Alexander found two pots of paint and some brushes in a corner, then the boys went off, leaving Lucy alone.

She stood looking at the furniture, at the statues, at the sarcophagus... which had a heavy, close-fitting lid. She looked around and on the floor found a big <u>crowbar</u>.

It was not easy, but she worked with determination and slowly the lid began to rise, enough for Lucy to see what was inside...

CHAPTER 6

A few minutes later she left the barn, locked the door, put the key back on the nail, then drove down to the telephone box.

'I want to speak to Miss Marple.'

'She's resting, and I'm not going to wake her.'

'You must wake her. It's urgent.'

Florence did not argue any more. Soon Miss Marple's voice spoke. 'Yes, Lucy?'

'I've found it.'

'A woman's body?'

'Yes. A woman in a fur coat. It's in a sarcophagus in a barn near the house. I think I ought to inform the police.'

'Yes. You must inform the police.'

'But the first thing they'll want to know is *why* I was lifting up that great heavy lid. Do you want me to invent a reason?'

'No,' said Miss Marple, 'you must tell the truth.'

'About you?'

'About everything.'

Lucy suddenly smiled. 'That will be easy for me!' She said goodbye and rang the police station. Then she drove back to Rutherford Hall and went to the library, where Miss Crackenthorpe was reading to her father.

'Can I speak to you, Miss Crackenthorpe?'

Emma looked up, a little nervously.

'Well, speak up, girl, speak up,' said old Mr Crackenthorpe.

Lucy said to Emma, 'I'd like to speak to you alone, please.'

'Just a moment, Father.' Emma got up and went out into the hall. Lucy followed her and shut the door behind them.

Emma said, 'If you think there's too much work with the boys here, I can help you and—'

'It's not that,' said Lucy. 'But I didn't want to speak before your father because it might give him a shock. You see, I've just discovered the body of a murdered woman in that sarcophagus in the Long Barn.'

'In the sarcophagus? A murdered woman? It's impossible!'

'I'm afraid it's true. I've told the police. They will be here very soon.'

Emma's face went a little red. 'You should have told me first – before telling the police.'

'I'm sorry,' said Lucy, as they heard the sound of a car outside and the doorbell rang through the house.

II

'I'm very sorry to have asked you to do this,' said Inspector Bacon as he led Emma Crackenthorpe out of the barn.

Emma's face was pale, but she walked steadily. 'I have never seen the woman before.'

'Thank you, Miss Crackenthorpe. That's all I wanted to know.'

'I must go to my father. I telephoned Dr Quimper as soon as I heard about this.'

Dr Quimper came out of the library as they crossed the hall. He was a tall friendly-looking man. 'You were right to call me, Emma,' he said. 'Your father's all right. Just go in and see him, then get yourself a glass of <u>brandy</u>. That's doctor's orders.'

Emma smiled at him gratefully and went into the library.

'She's one of the best,' he said, looking after her. 'A pity she never married.'

'She cares too much for her father, I suppose,' said Inspector Bacon.

'She doesn't care that much – but her father likes being an <u>invalid</u>, so she lets him be an invalid. She's the same with her brothers. Cedric thinks he's a good painter, Harold believes he is good with money, and Alfred enjoys shocking her with his stories of his clever deals. Well, do you want me to have a look at the body now the police doctor has finished?'

'I'd like you to have a look, yes, Doctor. We want to get her identified. I suppose it's impossible for old Mr Crackenthorpe? It would upset him too much?'

'Upset him? Nonsense. He'd never forgive you if you didn't let him have a look. It's the most exciting thing that's happened to him for years – *and* it won't cost him anything!'

'There's nothing really wrong with him then?'

'He's seventy-two. That's all that's wrong with him. Come on, let's go and see this body of yours. Unpleasant, I suppose?'

'The police doctor says she's been dead for two or three weeks.'

'Very unpleasant, then.'

Dr Quimper stood by the sarcophagus and looked down at the body. 'I've never seen her before. She must have been quite good-looking once. Who found her?'

'Miss Lucy Eyelesbarrow.'

They went out again into the fresh air.

'What was *she* doing, looking inside a sarcophagus?'

'That,' said Inspector Bacon, 'is just what I am going to ask her. Now, about Mr Crackenthorpe. Will you—?'

'Disgusting!' Mr Crackenthorpe came out of the house. 'I brought back that sarcophagus from Rome in 1908 – or was it 1909?'

'Calm yourself,' the doctor said. 'This isn't going to be nice, you know.'

'I may be ill, but I've got to do my duty, haven't I?'

A very short visit inside the Long Barn was, however, long enough. Mr Crackenthorpe came out into the air again with surprising speed. 'I've never seen her before! It wasn't Rome – I remember now – it was Naples. A very fine example. And some stupid woman is found dead in it!' He put a hand on his chest. 'Oh, my heart… Doctor…'

Dr Quimper took his arm. 'You'll be all right after you have had a small brandy.' They went back together towards the house.

'And now,' Bacon said to himself, 'for Miss Lucy Eyelesbarrow!'

III

Lucy had just finished preparing potatoes for dinner when she was informed that Inspector Bacon wanted to see her. So she followed the policeman to a room where he was waiting.

'Now, Miss Eyelesbarrow,' Inspector Bacon said. 'You went into the Long Barn to find some paint. Is that right? And after you found the paint you forced up the lid of this sarcophagus and found the body. What were you looking for in the sarcophagus?'

'I was looking for a body,' said Lucy.

'You were looking for a body – and you found one! Doesn't that seem to you a very extraordinary story?'

'Oh, yes, it is an extraordinary story.' And Lucy told it to him.

The Inspector was shocked. 'Are you telling me that you were asked by an old lady to get a job here and to search the house and grounds for *a dead body*?'

'Yes.'

'Who is this old lady?'

'Miss Jane Marple. She is at the moment living at 4 Madison Road.'

The Inspector wrote it down. 'Do you really expect me to believe this?'

Lucy said, 'Not, perhaps, until after you have spoken to Miss Marple.'

'I shall speak to her all right. She must be mad.'

Lucy did not reply to this. Instead she said, 'What are you going to tell Miss Crackenthorpe? About *me*?'

'Why do you ask?'

'Well, I've done what I came here for. But I'm still supposed to be working for Miss Crackenthorpe, and there are two hungry boys in the house and probably some more of the family will arrive after all this upset. She needs help, but if you tell her that I only took this job in order to hunt for dead bodies, she'll probably tell me to leave.'

The Inspector looked hard at her. 'I'm not saying anything to anyone at present, because I don't yet know whether your statement is true.'

Lucy got up. 'Thank you. Then I'll go back to the kitchen and get on with things.'

CHAPTER 7

'So, you think we should ask the police in London to help us with this?' The <u>Chief Constable</u> looked at Inspector Bacon. 'You think we should speak to Scotland Yard?'

'The woman wasn't from the local area, sir,' Bacon said. 'We believe – because of her underwear – that she might have been foreign. But of course I'm not saying anything about that until after the <u>inquest</u>[7] tomorrow. Other members of the Crackenthorpe family will be here for it and there's a chance one of them might be able to identify her.'

'There is no reason, is there, to believe the Crackenthorpe family are connected with the crime in any way?' the Chief Constable asked.

'Not apart from the fact that the body was found on their land,' said Inspector Bacon. 'What I can't understand is this nonsense about the train.'

'Ah, yes. You've been to see this old lady, this – er—'

'Miss Marple, sir. Yes, she's certain about what her friend saw. I'm sure she's just imagining it, but she *did* ask this young woman to look for a body – which she did.'

'*And* found one,' said the Chief Constable. 'Miss Jane Marple – the name seems familiar somehow… Anyway, I'll speak to Scotland Yard. I think you are right about it not being a local case.'

II

The inquest was a formal affair. No one came forward to identify the dead woman. Lucy was asked to <u>give evidence</u> of finding the body and medical evidence was given about the cause of death – she had been strangled.[6]

It was a cold, windy day when the Crackenthorpe family came out of the hall. There were five of them, Emma, Cedric, Harold, Alfred, and Bryan Eastley, the husband of the dead daughter, Edith. There was also Mr Wimborne, the family's London lawyer. They all stood for a moment on the pavement. A small crowd had gathered there; the story of the 'Body in the Sarcophagus' had been fully reported in both the London and the local Press.

Voices were heard saying, 'That's them...'

Emma said sharply, 'Let's get away.' She got into the big hired car with Lucy. Mr Wimborne, Cedric and Harold followed.

Bryan Eastley said, 'I'll take Alfred in my car.'

The Daimler was about to leave when Emma cried, 'Oh, stop! There are the boys!'

Alexander and James had been left behind at Rutherford Hall, but now they suddenly appeared. 'We came on our bicycles,' said Stoddart-West. 'The policeman was very kind and let us in at the back of the hall.'

'But it was rather disappointing,' said Alexander. 'All over so soon.'

'We can't stay here talking,' said Harold angrily. 'There's all those men with cameras.' He gave a sign to the driver, who drove away down the road.

'All over so soon!' said Cedric. 'That's what they think, the young <u>innocents</u>! It's just beginning.'

'It's most unfortunate,' Harold said. 'By the way Miss – er – Eyelesbarrow, *why* were you looking in that sarcophagus?'

They all looked at Lucy. She had wondered when one of the family would ask her this and had already prepared her answer. 'I don't know... I *did* feel that the whole place needed to be cleaned. And there was...' she paused, 'a very unpleasant smell...'

Mr Wimborne said, 'Yes, yes, of course... but this unfortunate young woman was nothing to do with any of us.'

'Ah, but you can't be so sure of that, can you?' said Cedric.

Lucy looked at him with interest. She had already noticed that the three brothers were very different. Cedric was a big man with untidy dark hair and a cheerful manner. He was still wearing the clothes in which he had arrived from the airport; old grey trousers, and an old brown jacket. He looked <u>bohemian</u> and proud of it.

His brother Harold was the opposite; the perfect picture of a City gentleman. He was tall, with smooth, dark hair, and was dressed in a suit and a pale grey tie. He said, 'Really, Cedric, that seems a *most* unnecessary remark.'

'Why? She was in our barn, so what did she come there for?'

Mr Wimborne coughed. 'Possibly some – er – romantic meeting. I have heard that all the locals knew that the key was kept outside on a nail.'

Emma said, 'Yes, it was for the Women's Institute people.'

Mr Wimborne coughed again. 'It seems probable that the barn was used in the winter by local lovers. There was a disagreement and some young man lost control of himself. Then he saw the sarcophagus and he realized that it would make an excellent hiding place.'

'If I was a girl coming to meet my young man, I wouldn't like being taken to a freezing cold barn,' Cedric replied. 'I'd want a nice warm cinema, wouldn't you, Miss Eyelesbarrow?'

'Do we really need to discuss all this?' Harold said.

But as he asked the question, the car stopped outside the front door of Rutherford Hall.

CHAPTER 8

As he entered the library Mr Wimborne looked past Inspector Bacon whom he had already met, to the fair-haired, good-looking man behind him.

'This is Detective Inspector Craddock of Scotland Yard,' Inspector Bacon said.

Dermot Craddock smiled at Mr Wimborne. 'As you are representing the Crackenthorpe family, I think that we should give you some <u>confidential</u> information. We believe that the dead woman travelled down here from London and that she had recently come from abroad. Probably from France. Now I would like to have a quick talk with each member of the family...'

'I really cannot see...'

'What they can tell me? Probably nothing. I expect I can get most of the information I want from you. Information about this house and the family.'

'And how can that possibly be connected with an unknown woman coming from abroad and being killed here?'

'Well, that's the question,' said Craddock. 'Why did she come here? Had she once had some connection with this house? Had she been, perhaps, a servant here? Or did she come to meet someone else who had lived at Rutherford Hall? Can you give me a short history of the family?'

'There is very little to tell,' said Wimborne. 'Josiah Crackenthorpe made sweet and savoury biscuits. He became very rich. He built this house. Luther Crackenthorpe, his eldest son, lives here now.'

'And the present Mr Crackenthorpe has never thought of selling the house?'

'He is unable to do so,' said the lawyer. 'Because of his father's will.'[8]

'Perhaps you'll tell me about the will?'

'Josiah Crackenthorpe left his great fortune in trust,[8] the income from it to be paid to his son Luther for life, and after Luther's death, the capital to be divided equally between Luther's children, Edmund, Cedric, Harold, Alfred, Emma and Edith. Edmund was killed in the war, and Edith died four years ago, so that on Luther Crackenthorpe's death, the money will be divided between Cedric, Harold, Alfred, Emma and Edith's son Alexander Eastley.'

'And the house?'

'That will go to Luther Crackenthorpe's eldest living son or his children.'

'Was Edmund Crackenthorpe married?'

'No.'

'So the property will actually go—?'

'To the next son – Cedric,' said Mr Wimborne.

'So at present the next generation have no income except what they make or what their father gives them, and their father has a large income but no control of the capital.'[8]

'Exactly.' Mr Wimborne stood up. 'I'm now going back to London. Unless there is anything more you wish to know.'

II

Lucy had gone straight to the kitchen when she got back from the inquest, and was busy preparing lunch when Bryan Eastley came in.

'Can I help in any way?' he asked.

Lucy gave him a quick look. Bryan had arrived alone at the inquest in his small M.G. sports car, and she had not had much time to study him. She now saw a friendly-looking man, about thirty years old, with fair hair and blue eyes.

'The boys aren't back yet,' he said, sitting on the end of the kitchen table.

Lucy smiled. 'They were determined not to miss anything. Do you mind getting off the table, Mr Eastley? I want to put this hot dish down there.'

Bryan obeyed. 'Do you mind me talking to you?'

'If you came in to help, I'd rather you helped.' Lucy took another dish from the oven. 'Here – turn all these potatoes over so that they will get brown on the other side.'

Bryan did as he was told. Then he watched Lucy pour the <u>Yorkshire pudding</u> mixture into the dish. 'This is fun. It reminds me of being in our kitchen at home – when I was a boy.'

There was something strangely sad about Bryan Eastley, Lucy thought. Looking closely at him, she realized that he must be nearer forty than thirty. He reminded her of the many young pilots she had known during the war when she had been only fourteen. She had gone on and grown up into a world after the war– but she felt that Bryan had not gone on, but had been left behind. She remembered what Emma had told her. 'You were a fighter pilot, weren't you? You've got a medal.'[4]

'Yes, and if you've got a medal, people try to make things easy for you. They give you a job, which is very good of them. But they're all office jobs, and I'm just not any good at that sort of thing. I've had ideas of my own but… If I had a bit of capital…' He paused.

At that moment Alexander and Stoddart-West arrived.

'Hello, Bryan,' said Alexander to his father. 'Oh, what a good piece of meat. Is there Yorkshire pudding?'

'Yes, there is,' said Lucy.

'She's an excellent cook.' Alexander spoke to Bryan like a kindly father to his son.

'Can we help you, Miss Eyelesbarrow?' asked Stoddart-West.

'Yes, you can. Alexander, go and ring the bell. James, will you carry this dish into the <u>dining room</u>? And will you take the meat in, Mr Eastley? I'll bring the potatoes and the Yorkshire pudding.'

When Lucy came out into the hall, Mr Wimborne was standing there putting on his coat, Emma was coming down the stairs, and two police officers were coming out of the library.

Mr Wimborne took Emma's hand in his. 'Now this is Detective Inspector Craddock from Scotland Yard who has come to take charge of the case. And he has just told me that this almost certainly was not a local crime. They think she came from London and was probably foreign.'

Emma Crackenthorpe said sharply, 'Was she French?'

Chapter 9

After lunch, the police officers asked if they could talk to Mr Cedric Crackenthorpe. Inspector Craddock said, 'I hear you have just come from Ibiza? You live out there?'

'It's better than this boring country.'

'You get more sunshine than we do, I expect,' said Inspector Craddock. 'But you came home not very long ago – for Christmas. What made you come back again so soon?'

Cedric smiled. 'I got a call from my sister. We've never had a murder here before and I didn't want to miss anything. Also I thought poor Emma might need a bit of help – managing the old man and the police and everything.'

'I see. Although her two other brothers have also come to be with her.'

'But not to cheer her up,' Cedric said. 'Harold is very angry about it. It's not at all suitable for a City man to be mixed up with the murder of a strange female.'

'Was she – a strange female?' Inspector Craddock asked. 'I thought perhaps you might be able to guess who she was?'

Cedric shook his head. 'I have no idea.'

Craddock leaned back in his chair. 'As you heard at the inquest, the time of death was between two and four weeks ago – which makes it somewhere around Christmas. When did you arrive in England and when did you leave?'

Cedric thought. 'I got here on the Saturday before Christmas – that would be the 21st.'

'You flew straight here?'

'Yes, and got here at midday. I flew back on the following Friday, the 27th.'

'Thank you.'

Cedric smiled. 'That puts me well within the time of the murder, unfortunately. But really, Inspector, strangling young women is not my favourite form of Christmas fun.'

'So what do you think of him?' Craddock asked Bacon as Cedric shut the door behind him.

'I don't like that type,' Bacon said. 'Dirty trousers, and did you see his tie? It looked as though it was made of coloured string. He's just the type who would strangle a woman and think nothing about it.'

'Well, he didn't strangle this one – if he didn't leave Ibiza until the 21st. And that's a thing we can easily check.'

Bacon looked at him. 'I notice that you're not telling them the actual date of the crime.'

'No, we'll keep quiet about that for a bit. Now we'll see what our correct City gentleman has to say about it all.'

Harold Crackenthorpe had very little to say about it. No, he had no idea who the dead woman was. Yes, he had been at Rutherford Hall for Christmas. He had been unable to come down until Christmas Eve – but had stayed on over the following weekend.

Inspector Craddock then asked to see Alfred, and when he came into the room Craddock felt that he had seen him somewhere before. He asked Alfred what job he did.

'I'm in insurance at the moment. Until recently I've been interested in putting a new type of talking machine on the market. I did very well out of that.'

Inspector Craddock smiled – but he was noticing how Alfred's suit, which had looked smart when he came in, was really very cheap. Cedric's clothes had been dirty, but they had been made of excellent material. Alfred's cheap but smart clothes told their own story. Craddock began to ask his usual questions and Alfred seemed interested.

'It's quite an idea, that the woman might once have had a job here. But as Emma didn't recognize her, I think that's unlikely. And if the woman came from London… What made you think she came from London, by the way?'

Inspector Craddock smiled and shook his head.

'Not telling, eh?' Alfred said. 'Did she have a return ticket in her coat pocket, is that it?'

Inspector Craddock thanked Alfred and let him go.

II

'I don't suppose you want to see me,' said Bryan Eastley, coming into the room. 'I don't really belong to the family.'

'You were the husband of Miss Edith Crackenthorpe, who died five years ago?' Inspector Craddock asked.

'That's right.'

'Well, it's very kind of you, Mr Eastley, especially if you know something that could help us.'

'But I don't. I wish I did. Is it true that she was foreign?'

'She may have been French,' said Inspector Bacon.

Bryan's blue eyes suddenly looked interested. 'Really?'

Inspector Craddock said, 'Has anybody in the family got any French connections, that you know of?'

Bryan shook his head. 'I'm not being very helpful, am I?' He smiled. 'But Alexander and James are out every day hunting for clues. They'll probably find something for you.'

Inspector Craddock said he hoped they would, then said he would like to speak to Miss Emma Crackenthorpe.

III

Inspector Craddock looked more carefully at Emma Crackenthorpe than he had done before. He was still wondering about the expression on her face before lunch when Wimborne had said the murdered woman was foreign.

'As you have heard, we believe the dead woman came from abroad which makes it more difficult for us to identify her.'

'But didn't she have anything – a handbag? Papers?'

Craddock shook his head.

'You have no idea of her name – of where she came from – anything at all?'

She's very anxious to know who the woman is, Craddock thought.

'We know nothing about her,' he said. 'Can you think of anyone she might be?'

'I have no idea at all.'

Inspector Craddock's voice was hard as he asked, 'When Mr Wimborne told you that the woman was foreign, why did you assume that she was French?'

Emma remained calm. 'Did I? I don't really know why – except that most foreigners in this country *are* French, aren't they?'

'Oh, I really don't think so, Miss Crackenthorpe. People from so many countries come here, Italians, Germans, Belgians...' Craddock looked at Inspector Bacon who showed her a small powder compact. 'Do you recognize this, Miss Crackenthorpe?'

'No. It's not mine.'

'You've no idea whose it is?'

'No.'

'Then I don't think we need worry you any more – for the present.'

'Thank you.' She smiled, got up, and left the room.

'Do you think she knows anything?' asked Bacon.

Inspector Craddock said, 'I often think that everyone knows more than they want to tell you, but...'

But suddenly the door was thrown open and old Mr Crackenthorpe came in, looking very angry. 'So Scotland Yard comes here and doesn't have the good manners to talk to the head of the family first! Tell me, who is the Master of this house?'

'You are, of course, Mr Crackenthorpe,' said Craddock, standing up. 'But we thought that you had already told Inspector Bacon all you know, and as Dr Quimper said...'

'Yes, yes, I am not a strong man... but Dr Quimper is like a silly old woman sometimes. And there has been a murder in my own house – well, in my own barn! So, what do you want to know? What's your theory?'

'It's a bit early for theories, Mr Crackenthorpe. We are still trying to find out who the woman was.'

'Foreign, you say?'

'We think so.'

'And you think she was involved with one of my sons? If so, she would be Alfred's woman. And some violent man followed her down here, thinking she was coming to meet Alfred and killed her. How's that?'

'But Mr Alfred Crackenthorpe did not recognize her,' Inspector Craddock said.

'He's a liar, always was!' And he left the room.

'Alfred's woman?' said Bacon. 'I don't think Alfred is who we're looking for – but I did just wonder about that Air Force man.'

'Bryan Eastley?'

'Yes. I've met one or two like him. They had danger and death and excitement too early. Now they find life boring and they don't mind risking things.[4] If Eastley were mixed up with a woman and wanted to kill her…' He stopped 'But if you do kill a woman, why put her in your father-in-law's sarcophagus? No, none of this family had anything to do with the murder.' Bacon stood up. 'Anything more you want to do here?'

Craddock said there wasn't, so he was going to call on an old friend.

CHAPTER 10

Miss Marple, sitting very straight on Florence's sofa, smiled at Inspector Dermot Craddock. 'I'm so glad that you have been asked to help with the case. I hoped you would be.'

'When I got your letter,' said Craddock, 'I took it straight to the A.C., the Assistant Commissioner. And he had just heard from the Brackhampton people asking for our help. The A.C. was very interested in what I had to tell him about you. He had heard about you from my godfather.'

'Dear Sir Henry,' said Miss Marple.

'So he sent me to look into the case, and here I am! Of course, this meeting is not an official one. I'm hoping you can put yourself in the murderer's place, and tell me where he is now?'

Miss Marple shook her head. 'I wish I could. But I've no idea. Although he must be someone who knows all about Rutherford Hall.'

'I agree. But that includes so many people. A lot of women have worked there. And there's the Women's Institute and other groups. They all know the Long Barn and where the key was kept. Also we'll never begin to solve the crime until we identify the body.'

'And that, too, may be difficult?'

'Oh, we'll get there – in the end. We're checking up on all disappearances of a woman of that age. Her fur coat is a cheap one bought in London. Most of her other clothes were bought in Paris.'

'The powder compact wasn't any help?'

'Unfortunately, no. Hundreds of them are sold in Paris. Have you any more ideas for me?'

'I was thinking about theatrical companies,' said Miss Marple. 'Moving from place to place. One of those young women would be much less likely to be missed.'

CHAPTER 11

'I can't understand you.' Cedric Crackenthorpe stepped down from the wall of an old <u>pigsty</u> and looked at Lucy Eyelesbarrow.

'What can't you understand?'

'What you're doing here?'

'I'm doing my job.'

'As a *servant*?'

'Servant, indeed! I'm a Professional Household Help.'

'You can't like all the things you have to do.'

Lucy laughed. 'Not everything, perhaps, but cooking satisfies my wish to be creative, and I really enjoy making things tidy.'

'I don't like things to be tidy,' said Cedric.

'Yes, I can see that.'

Some bricks fell out of the pigsty and Cedric turned to look inside it. 'Dear old Madge used to live here. She was such a friendly animal and such a good mother. We used to come here and scratch her back with a stick. She loved it.'

'Why has this whole place been allowed to get into such a state? It can't only be the war.'

'You'd like to tidy this up, too, I suppose?' He paused. 'No, it's not only the war. It's my father. He refuses to spend any money on the place. Of course he hates all of us – except perhaps Emma. That's because of my grandfather's will. Although now he's got nearly as big a fortune as my grandfather left, while all of us...' He stopped as Emma came through the door of the kitchen garden. 'Hello, Emma. You're looking a bit upset.'

'I want to talk to you, Cedric.'

'I must get back to the house,' said Lucy.

Cedric's eyes followed her as she walked away. 'Good-looking girl. Who is she really?'

'Oh, she's quite well-known,' said Emma. 'But forget Lucy Eyelesbarrow, the police think that the dead woman was foreign, perhaps French. Cedric, you don't think she could possibly be – *Martine*?'

II

For a moment or two Cedric just looked at her. '*Martine*?'

'Yes. She sent that <u>telegram</u> at about the same time… Do you think she might, after all, have come down here and…'

'Nonsense. Why would Martine come down here and go to the Long Barn?'

'You don't think, perhaps, that I ought to tell Inspector Bacon – or the other one?'

'Tell him what?'

'Well – about Martine. About her letter.'

'Now don't start making things complicated, Emma. I was never sure that letter was from Martine, anyway.'

'I was. And I really *am* worried. I don't know what I ought to do.'

'Nothing,' said Cedric. 'Never go forward to meet trouble, that's my advice.'

Emma turned and went slowly back to the house. As she reached the drive, Dr Quimper came out and walked towards her.

'Well, Emma, murder has given your father a new interest in life. I must tell that to my other patients.'

Emma smiled but her eyes remained troubled.

'Is something wrong?' Dr Quimper asked.

'I am worried, yes.'

'Do you want to tell me about it?'

'Yes, because I don't know what to do. You remember what I once told you about my brother Edmund – the one who was killed in the war?'

'You mean that he had married – or had wanted to marry – a French girl?'

'Yes. Almost immediately after I got that letter, he was killed. We never heard anything about the girl. All we knew was her first name. We thought she would contact us, but she didn't. We never heard *anything* – until about a month ago, just before Christmas.'

'You got a letter, didn't you?'

'Yes. Saying she was in England and would like to come and see us. It was all arranged and then, suddenly, she sent a message that she had to return to France.'

'Well?'

'The police think that the murdered woman – was French.'

'They do, do they? Are you worried that she might be your brother's girl?'

'Yes.'

'I think it's unlikely,' said Dr Quimper.

'I'm wondering if I ought to tell the police about it all. Cedric and the others say it's unnecessary. What do you think?'

Dr Quimper was silent for a moment, then he said, 'It's much *simpler* if you say nothing. I can understand what your brothers feel about it. But...'

'Yes?'

He looked at her and smiled. 'I would just tell them. You'll keep worrying if you don't. I know you.'

Emma's face went a little pink. 'I'm probably being silly.'

'You do what you want to do, Emma – and forget the rest of your family! I would back your judgment against them any day.'

CHAPTER 12

'Girl! You, girl! Come in here.'

Lucy turned her head, surprised. Old Mr Crackenthorpe was calling to her loudly from a small room. He took hold of her arm and pulled her inside. 'I want to show you something.'

Lucy looked round her. 'Do you want me to clean this room?' They were in a study, but there were piles of dusty papers on the desk and spiders in corners of the ceiling.

Old Mr Crackenthorpe shook his head. 'No! I keep it locked up. It's *my* room. See these stones? They're very old.'

Lucy looked at the piles of stones. 'Most interesting.'

'You're a clever girl. They are interesting. I'll show you some more things.'

'It's very kind of you, but I really have a lot to do. With six people in the house—'

'Costing me a fortune in food. That's all they do when they come down here! Eat. All waiting for me to die. Emma thinks I'm an old man. You don't think I'm old, do you?'

'Of course not,' said Lucy.

'Sensible girl. Now, I'm going to show you something.' He took a key from his pocket and unlocked the door of a dark wooden cupboard. From this he took out a surprisingly new-looking money box, which he also unlocked. 'Do you know what these are, my dear?' He took out some gold coins. '<u>Sovereigns</u>.[8] Worth a lot more than silly pieces of paper. Emma doesn't know – nobody knows. It's our secret, see, girl? Do you know why I'm telling you?'

'Why?'

'Because there's still lots of life in me and you're a <u>spirited</u> girl, so don't throw yourself away on a young man. Young men are stupid!

You *wait...*' His fingers pressed into Lucy's arm. '*Wait.* I'm going to live longer than all of my children. And then we'll see! Oh, yes. Harold's got no children. Cedric and Alfred aren't married. Emma – she'll never marry now. She rather likes Quimper – but Quimper will never marry Emma. There's Alexander, of course. Yes, there's Alexander... I'm fond of Alexander...' He paused looking worried. 'Well, girl, what about it?'

'Miss Eyelesbarrow!' Emma's voice came faintly through the closed door.

Lucy said quickly, 'Miss Crackenthorpe's calling me. I must go...'

'Don't forget – our secret...'

'I won't forget,' said Lucy, and hurried out into the hall, not sure whether or not Mr Crackenthorpe had just asked her to marry him.

II

Dermot Craddock sat at his desk at Scotland Yard talking into the telephone, in French. 'It was only an idea, you understand.' 'Yes,' said the voice from the Paris police. 'And already we have two or three possibilities. It is a pity that the photograph you sent me is so difficult for anyone to recognize. But I will continue to make inquiries.'

As Craddock said goodbye, a piece of paper was placed on his desk. It said:

Miss Emma Crackenthorpe.

To see Detective Inspector Craddock.

As Emma came in he offered her a chair. 'Miss Crackenthorpe, you have been worried about something, haven't you? Do you perhaps think you know who the dead woman was?'

'No, no, not really that. But...' Emma paused. 'You have met three of my brothers. I had another brother, Edmund, who was killed in the war. Just before he was killed, he wrote to me from France.' She opened her handbag, took out a letter and read from it:

I hope this won't be a shock to you, Emma, but I'm getting married – to a French girl. I know you'll like Martine – and look after her if anything happens to me. Please be careful how you tell Father. He'll probably go mad.

She continued, 'Two days after receiving this, we had a message saying Edmund was *Missing, believed killed*. Later he was definitely reported killed. It was just before <u>Dunkirk</u> – and a time of great confusion. There was no Army record of his marriage so I was very surprised to receive a letter just about a month ago, signed *Martine Crackenthorpe*.'

'Do you have it?'

Emma took the letter from her bag and handed it to Craddock who read it.

Dear Mademoiselle,

I hope it will not be a shock to you to get this letter. I do not even know if your brother Edmund told you that we were married. He was killed only a few days afterwards. After the war ended, I decided that I would not contact you. I had made a new life for myself. But now things have changed. It is for my son that I write this letter. He is your brother's son, you see, and I can no longer give him the advantages he ought to have. I am coming to England early next week. Will you tell me if I can come and see you? My address for letters is 126 Elvers Crescent, N10.

Yours sincerely,
Martine Crackenthorpe

Craddock gave the letter back to Emma. 'What did you do when you received this?'

'I wrote to the address she gave, and invited her to come down to Rutherford Hall. A few days later I received a message from London: *Very sorry, had to return to France unexpectedly. Martine.* There were no more letters.'

'All this happened – when?'

'Just before Christmas.'

'And you believe that the woman whose body was found in the sarcophagus might be this Martine?'

'No, of course I don't. But when you said she was probably foreign – well, I couldn't help wondering...'

Craddock said, 'You were quite right to tell me about this. We'll make some inquiries.' He paused. 'Did you tell your father and your brothers about the letter?'

'I had to tell my father, of course. He got very angry.' She smiled faintly. 'He was sure it was all made up to get money out of us. I also told my brothers. Harold thought it was made up, too and that I should be very careful. Alfred thought the same, but also that it was rather funny. Cedric just wasn't interested. But we all thought that the family should meet Martine, and that our lawyer, Mr Wimborne, should be with us.'

'Did you try to contact her after you received the message?'

'Yes. I wrote to the address in London with *Please forward* on the envelope, but I have had no reply.'

'Rather a strange business...' He looked at her sharply. 'What were your feelings about it, if this girl really *was* your brother's widow?'

Emma's face <u>softened</u>. 'Edmund was my favourite brother, so it seemed right for Martine to ask his family for help as he had wanted her to do. The letter seemed real to me – but, as Harold

49

said, if it was written by someone pretending to be Martine, they must have known her very well for people to believe the letter came from her. But still…' She stopped.

'You wanted it to be true?' said Craddock gently.

'Yes, I wanted it to be true. I would be so happy if Edmund had left a son.'

Craddock nodded. 'As you say, the letter sounds genuine. What *is* surprising is what followed. You had replied kindly to her, so why, even if she had to go back to France, did she not write again? That is if she really was Edmund's widow. Did perhaps one of your brothers make inquiries that frightened her? But of course, if Edmund Crackenthorpe left a son, he would be one of the heirs to your grandfather's <u>estate</u>.'

Emma nodded.

'Well, don't worry. There is probably no connection at all between the woman who wrote the letter and the woman whose body was found in the sarcophagus.'

Emma stood up. 'I'm so glad I told you.'

When she had gone, Craddock rang for Detective Sergeant Wetherall. 'Bob, I want you to go to 126 Elvers Crescent, N10. Take photographs of the dead woman with you. Ask about a woman calling herself Mrs Martine Crackenthorpe who was either living there, or calling for letters there, between the 15th to the end of December.'

'Right, sir.'

Craddock was <u>occupied</u> with other matters for the rest of the day but when he returned to his office, he found a message from Paris on his desk.

Details given by you might fit Anna Stravinska of Ballet Maritski. Suggest you come over. Dessin.

Craddock smiled. At last! Forget Martine Crackenthorpe. He would go to Paris tonight.

CHAPTER 13

'It's so very kind of you to have asked me to tea,' said Miss Marple to Emma Crackenthorpe.

Looking like a picture of a sweet old lady, she smiled round her – at Harold in his dark suit, at Alfred handing her sandwiches, at Cedric standing by the fire wearing a very old jacket.

'We are pleased that you could come,' said Emma politely.

This wasn't really true. When she had said to her brothers, 'Oh, I told Miss Eyelesbarrow that she could bring her aunt to tea today,' they had not been pleased.

'Tell her not to come,' said Harold. 'We've still got a lot to talk about and don't want strangers here.'

'Let her have tea in the kitchen with the girl,' said Alfred.

'Oh, let her come,' said Cedric. 'We can ask her about the wonderful Lucy. I'm not sure that I trust her. She's much too clever.'

'She's quite genuine, I've made inquiries about her,' said Harold, then added, 'Emma, you must have been mad, telling the police that the dead woman might be Edmund's French wife. It will make them think that one of *us* killed her.'

'I told her not to,' said Cedric. 'Then Dr Quimper encouraged her to tell them.'

'And now this old woman is coming to tea. Just when we want to *think*,' said Harold.

But Miss Marple now sat by the fire smiling up at Emma. 'What a beautiful house you have. And how delightful to have your brothers with you. So often families are separated.'

'Tell us about Lucy as a child, Miss Marple,' said Cedric.

'Lucy was always so clever,' she said. 'Yes, you were, dear – particularly at mathematics. Why, I remember when the butcher charged me too much for a chicken…'

Miss Marple's memories were interrupted by Bryan and the boys coming in. Then tea was brought and with it came Dr Quimper.

'I hope your father's not ill, Emma?'

'Oh, no – he was just a little tired this afternoon.'

'Avoiding visitors, I expect,' said Miss Marple with a smile.

Dr Quimper, who was eating coffee cake with great enthusiasm said, 'What a good cook you are, Emma!'

'Not mine. Miss Eyelesbarrow's.'

'The ones you make are just as good,' said Quimper loyally.

'Will you come and see Father?' She got up and the doctor followed her.

Miss Marple watched them leave the room. 'Miss Crackenthorpe is a very loving daughter.'

'I can't imagine why,' said Cedric.

'Father cares about her very much,' said Harold quickly.

'Well, he knows that Emma will always take care of him. She'll never get married.'

Miss Marple's eyes widened. 'Really? I think that Miss Crackenthorpe will probably marry late in life – and successfully.'

'That's not very likely living here,' said Cedric. 'She never meets anybody she could marry.'

Miss Marple's eyes widened even more. 'There are always vicars – and doctors.' She looked at each of them and it was clear that what she had suggested did not please them. She stood up. 'So kind of you to invite me. I've been wondering just what your home was like – so that I can imagine dear Lucy working here.'

II

Lucy took Miss Marple home. On her way back, a figure stepped out of the darkness and stood into the light from the car just as she was turning into the back lane. He held up his hand and Lucy recognized Alfred Crackenthorpe.

'That's better,' he said, as he got in. 'Rutherford Hall is so dull. I thought I'd like a nice walk, but it's cold! How do you manage staying here, Lucy? You don't mind if I call you Lucy, do you?'

'Not at all. I don't find it dull.'

'But you're a clever girl. Too clever to waste yourself cooking and cleaning.'

'Thank you, but I prefer cooking and cleaning to office work.'

'But you could do something much more exciting.'

'Like what?'

'Well, I could use you in my business.' His hand touched her arm. 'You're a very beautiful girl. I'd like you as a partner.'

'Thank you.' Lucy drove the car into the yard and stopped.

'You mean, no. But think about it. I'll get some money quite soon. My father can't live for ever. What about it, Lucy?'

'What are the <u>terms</u>?'

'Marriage if you like.'

'Oh.' She laughed and opened the car door. 'This is no time for romance. There's dinner to think about.'

They entered the house and Lucy hurried to the kitchen.

After dinner, she came out into the hall to find Harold Crackenthorpe waiting for her.

'Miss Eyelesbarrow, can I speak to you about something?' He opened the door of the sitting room and she followed him in. 'I shall be leaving early in the morning, but I want to tell you that I feel that you are too good to be working here.'

'Do you? I don't.' Well, *he* can't ask me to marry him, thought Lucy. He's got a wife already.

'When you have finished here, come and see me in London. We could use someone of your ability in the company and I can offer you a very good salary.'

Lucy said, 'Thank you, Mr Crackenthorpe, I'll think about it.'

'Don't wait too long or you might miss the opportunity. Good night, Miss Eyelesbarrow.'

Then on her way up to bed, Lucy met Cedric on the stairs.

'Lucy, there's something I want to say to you.'

'Do you want me to marry you and come to Ibiza and look after you?'

Cedric looked very surprised. 'No.'

'Sorry. My mistake.'

'I just wanted to know if you have a train timetable in the house?'

'Is that all? There's one on the hall table.'

'You know,' said Cedric, 'you shouldn't think everyone wants to marry you. You're a good-looking girl but not as good-looking as all that. In fact, you're the last girl in the world I would want to marry.'

'Really?' said Lucy. 'Perhaps you'd prefer me as a stepmother?'

'What?' Cedric looked at her.

'You heard me,' said Lucy, and went into her room and shut the door.

CHAPTER 14

Dermot Craddock had arrived at the Paris Police Station.

Armand Dessin said, 'I have a picture of the ballet dancers here – that is her, the fourth from the left – do you recognize her?'

A strangled young woman is not easy to recognize. 'It *could* be her,' Inspector Craddock said. 'What do you know about her?'

'Almost nothing,' Dessin said cheerfully. 'She was not important, you see. And the Ballet Maritski – it is not important, either. It has no famous <u>ballerinas</u>. But I will take you to see Madame Joilet who organizes it.'

Madame Joilet was a business-<u>like</u> Frenchwoman. 'I do not like the police!'

'No, no, Madame, you must not say that,' said Dessin. 'Now about this girl, Anna Stravinska.'

'What about her?' said Madame.

'Is she Russian?' asked Inspector Craddock.

'No. But they all give themselves Russian names. She did not dance well, she was not good-looking.'

'Was she French?'

'Perhaps. But she told me that she had an English husband.'

'Was he alive – or dead?'

'Dead, or he had left her. These girls – there is always some trouble with men.'

'When did you last see her?'

'I took my company to London for six weeks. Then we came back to France, but Anna did not come. She sent a message that she was going to live with her husband's family. I did not think it was true. I thought that she had met a man, you understand.'

Inspector Craddock nodded. 'When was this?'

'We returned to France the Sunday before Christmas. And Anna left two – or three – days before that.' Madame Joilet paused. 'Why do you want to find her?'

'We think she may have been murdered.'

Madame Joilet turned away. 'It happens. Ah, well! She was a good Catholic.'

'Did you know, Madame, if she had a son?'

'If so, I know nothing about it.'

Madame Joilet had nothing more to tell them. When they showed her the powder compact, she said Anna had one like that, but so had most of the other girls.

They then interviewed some of the girls who had worked with Anna.

'She liked to pretend things,' one of them said. 'She told stories about being a film star in Hollywood.'

Another girl said, 'In London, she talked about a very rich man who was going to take her on a holiday around the world, because she reminded him of his daughter who had died in a car accident.'

None of this was helpful. The only fact they knew was that on 19th December Anna Stravinska had decided not to return to France, and that on the 20th December a woman looking a little like her had travelled to Brackhampton by the 4.33 train and had been strangled. And if the woman in the sarcophagus was not Anna Stravinska, where was Anna now?

To that, Madame Joilet's answer was simple. 'With a man!'

And it was probably correct, Craddock thought. But there was one other possibility that had to be considered – because Anna had once said that she had an English husband. Had that husband been Edmund Crackenthorpe?

It seemed unlikely, considering Anna's character. What was much more probable was that Anna had known Martine and so it *might* have been Anna who wrote that letter to Emma Crackenthorpe.

II

When Craddock got back to the police station, Sergeant Wetherall was waiting with his report.

'126 Elvers Crescent is rented to students. Nobody could recognize the photograph as that of a woman who had called for letters.'

Craddock nodded. Then he rang up the Crackenthorpes' lawyers and asked for an appointment with Mr Wimborne.

The next day he was taken into a room where Mr Wimborne was sitting behind a large desk.

'What can I do for you, Inspector?'

'This letter…' Craddock pushed Martine's letter across the table.

Mr Wimborne looked at it. 'Yes, Miss Emma Crackenthorpe informed me about this yesterday morning. Extraordinary! I should have been asked about it when it arrived! I had never heard anything about Edmund getting married or having a son.'

'What would she and the son expect to <u>inherit</u>, legally – if she could prove her <u>claim</u>?' Craddock asked.

'Well, if she could prove that the boy was the son of Edmund Crackenthorpe, born after they were married, then he would receive his share of Josiah Crackenthorpe's money on the death of Luther Crackenthorpe. More than that, he would inherit Rutherford Hall, since he's the son of the eldest son.'

'Without that proof, when Luther Crackenthorpe dies, then Cedric gets it?'

'Yes, as the eldest living son.'

'But Harold and Alfred Crackenthorpe seem to have been more upset than Cedric by this letter. Is it true that they're both a bit short of money?' Craddock asked.

Mr Wimborne looked at him sharply. 'Oh! So the police have been making inquiries? Yes, Alfred is always short of money. And Harold is at present in some difficulty. But nobody's murdered Luther Crackenthorpe, which is the only murder that would do the family any good. So, really, Inspector, I don't see where your ideas are leading you.'

The worst of it was, Inspector Craddock thought, that he wasn't very sure himself.

CHAPTER 15

Inspector Craddock arranged to see Harold Crackenthorpe at his office, and went there with Sergeant Wetherall. The office was in the City and inside everything looked very expensive and business-like.

Harold was sitting behind a leather-topped desk in his private room. 'Good morning, Inspector. I hope this means that you have some real news for us at last?'

'I am afraid not, Mr Crackenthorpe. I'd just like to ask you a few more questions.'

'Well, what is it this time?'

'Could you tell me exactly what you were doing on the afternoon and evening of 20th December last – say between the hours of 3 pm and midnight.'

Crackenthorpe's face went an angry red. 'That seems to be a most extraordinary question.'

'It is a question for several other people as well as you,' said Craddock.

'Well, of course – I would like to help in any way I can.' He spoke into one of the telephones on his desk and a neat young woman entered. 'Miss Ellis, the Inspector would like to know what I was doing on the afternoon and evening of Friday 20th December.'

'Oh, yes.' Miss Ellis left the room, returned with a diary. 'You were in the office on the morning of 20th December. You had a meeting with Mr Goldie about the Cromartie business, you lunched with <u>Lord</u> Forthville—'

'Ah, it was that day, yes.'

'You returned to the office about three o'clock and later you went to <u>Sotheby's</u>[9] where you were interested in some rare books which were being sold that day. You did not return to the office, but you were attending the Catering Club dinner that evening.' Miss Ellis left the room.

'Yes,' said Harold. 'I went to Sotheby's but the books I wanted went for too high a price. I had tea in a small place in Jermyn Street – Russells, I think it was called, then went home – I live at 43 Cardigan Gardens. The Catering Club dinner was at seven-thirty, and after it I returned home to bed.'

'What time was it when you returned home to dress for the dinner, Mr Crackenthorpe?'

'Just after six, I think.'

'And after your dinner?'

'It was, I think, half past eleven when I got home.'

'Did a servant let you in? Or perhaps Lady Alice Crackenthorpe...?'

'My wife is in the South of France. I let myself in.'

'So there is no one who can say that you got home when you say you did?'

Harold gave him a cold look. 'I expect the servants heard me come in. But, really, Inspector—'

'Please, Mr Crackenthorpe, I know these questions are annoying, but I have nearly finished. Do you own a car?'

'Yes, but I don't use it much except at weekends.'

'But you use it when you go down to see your father and sister in Brackhampton?'

'Not unless I am going to stay there for a while. If I just go down for one night – as, for example, to the inquest – I always go by train.'

'Where do you keep your car?'

'I rent a garage behind Cardigan Gardens. Any more questions?'

'That's all for now,' said Inspector Craddock, smiling.

When they were outside, Sergeant Wetherall, said, 'He didn't like those questions at all.'

'If you have not committed a murder, it naturally annoys you if it seems someone thinks that you have,' said Inspector Craddock. 'But what we have to find out is if anyone saw Harold Crackenthorpe at the rare book sale that afternoon, and at the tea-shop. He could easily have travelled by the 4.33, pushed the woman out of the train and caught a train back to London in time to appear at the dinner. He could also have driven his car down that night, moved the body to the sarcophagus and driven back again. Make inquiries in the street where his garage is.'

'Yes, sir. Do you think that's what he did do?'

'How do I know?' asked Craddock. 'He's a tall, dark-haired man, like the one Miss Marple's friend saw on the train. Now for Brother Alfred.'

II

Alfred Crackenthorpe had a flat in West Hampstead, in a big modern building. But the flat was small, with just a table, a single bed, and some chairs. Craddock explained why he had come and asked Alfred what he had been doing on the afternoon and evening of 20th December.

'That's over three weeks ago. I never remember times or places. Except Christmas Day. Everyone knows where they were on Christmas Day, and I was with my father at Brackhampton.'

'And this year your father was ill, wasn't he?'

'Yes. Caused by eating and drinking more than he was used to.'

'But I heard that his doctor was – worried.'

'Ah, that stupid Quimper. It's no use listening to *him*.'

'He seemed a rather sensible man to me.'

'Well, he's not. So when father felt ill, Quimper was here all the time asking questions about everything he'd eaten and drunk. The whole thing was mad!'

Craddock didn't say anything, so Alfred asked angrily, '*Why* do you want to know where I was on a particular Friday, three or four weeks ago?'

'So you do remember that it was a Friday?'

'I thought you said it was.'

'Perhaps I did,' said Inspector Craddock. 'Anyway, Friday 20th is the day I am asking about.'

'Why? Have you found out something more about the murdered woman?'

'Our information is not yet complete.'

Alfred gave him a sharp look. 'I hope you don't believe this mad theory of Emma's that she might have been Edmund's widow. That's nonsense. Emma, of course, arranged a meeting with the woman.'

'Very wise,' said Craddock. 'Was there a date fixed for this meeting?'

'It was to be soon after Christmas – the weekend of the 27th...' he stopped.

'Ah,' said Craddock pleasantly. 'So you do remember some dates. But you can't tell me what you were doing on Friday 20th December?'

'Sorry – no. I probably just wandered around. Business gets done in bars more than anywhere else. I can't tell you what I was doing that day, but I can tell you what I *wasn't* doing. I wasn't murdering anyone in the Long Barn.'

'Why do you say that, Mr Crackenthorpe?'

'Come on, Inspector. You're investigating this murder, aren't you? Did somebody see the dead woman going into the barn that afternoon? She went in and she never came out? Is that it?'

The sharp black eyes were watching him, but Inspector Craddock said, 'I'm afraid we'll have to let you guess about that.'

'The police are so secretive.'

'Not only the police. I think, Mr Crackenthorpe, you *could* remember what you were doing on that Friday if you tried. Of course you may have reasons for not wishing to remember.' The inspector got up. 'I'm sorry you couldn't be more helpful, Mr Crackenthorpe.'

'*I'm* sorry too! It's all so silly. Even if the body is the body of Edmund's widow, why would any of us wish to kill her? We'd all have *enjoyed* making Father give her money and pay to send her son to a good school.'

III

'Sir, that <u>chap</u>, I've seen him before,' Sergeant Wetherall said. 'He was involved with Dicky Rogers and some of the <u>Soho</u> lot who stole jewellery.'

Of course! Craddock realized why Alfred's face had seemed familiar. They had all been small crimes, and nothing had ever been proved.

'Do you think he did it, sir?'

'I don't know. But it explains why he couldn't give himself an <u>alibi</u>.'

'So you think he's all right?'

'No one's all right just yet,' said Inspector Craddock.

CHAPTER 16

When Craddock got to 4 Madison Road, he found Lucy Eyelesbarrow with Miss Marple. 'I'm not on duty this afternoon, Miss Eyelesbarrow, so I've come to see the true expert on murder!'

Miss Marple looked at him and laughed. 'I told you, Lucy, Sir Henry Clithering, his godfather, is a very old friend of mine.'

'Yes, and he described her as the best detective in the world. Not only could she tell you what *might* have happened, and even what actually *did* happen! But also *why* it happened.'

Miss Marple's face was pink. 'Really... I just know a *little*, perhaps, about human nature... living, you know, in a *village*...'

'Do you feel that if you saw the person who had done the murder, you'd know?' asked Lucy.

'Oh, I wouldn't say *that*, dear. All one can do is to observe people and see of whom they remind you.'

'Like Cedric and the bank manager?'

'The bank manager's *son*, dear. Mr Eade himself was far more like Harold – a little too fond of money – the sort of man, too, who would do anything to avoid scandal.'

Craddock smiled. 'And who does Alfred remind you of?'

'Mr Jenkins at the garage. He didn't exactly steal tools, but he used to exchange a broken one for a good one. And Emma,' continued Miss Marple, 'she reminds me of Geraldine Webb – always very quiet – and bossed around by her elderly mother. It was a great surprise when the mother died and Geraldine went off on holiday, and came back married to a very nice lawyer.'

Lucy said, 'What you said about Emma marrying seemed to upset the brothers.'

Miss Marple nodded. 'Yes. So like men – unable to see what's going on in front of them. I don't think you noticed either.'

'No,' Lucy replied. 'They both seemed to me…'

'So old?' said Miss Marple. 'But Dr Quimper isn't much over forty. And Emma Crackenthorpe is under forty. The doctor's wife died young having a baby, so I have heard. He must be lonely.'

'Are we investigating crime, or are we arranging a marriage?' asked Lucy.

Miss Marple smiled. 'I'm afraid I *am* rather romantic. And now you have finished what you were doing for me at Rutherford Hall, if you really want a holiday…'

'And leave Rutherford Hall? Never! I'm the complete detective now. Almost as bad as Alexander and James. They spend all their time looking for clues. They looked all through the rubbish bins yesterday. So if they come to you, Inspector, with a bit of paper with *Martine – if you value your life keep away from the Long Barn!* on it, you'll know that I felt so sorry for them that I hid it in the pigsty!'

Inspector Craddock looked at her. 'Miss Eyelesbarrow, I'd like your opinion on something. What does the family think about this Martine business?'

'They're all furious with Emma for going to you about it,' Lucy replied. 'And with Dr Quimper, who encouraged her. Harold and Alfred think the letter wasn't really from Martine. Emma isn't sure. Cedric agrees with his brothers but he doesn't think it's as serious as they do. Bryan, though, seems sure that Martine wrote the letter.'

'Why, I wonder?'

'Well, Bryan just accepts things without question. He's rather sweet, like a dog that wants to be taken for a walk.'

'And do you take him for a walk, dear?' asked Miss Marple. 'To the pigsties, perhaps?'

Lucy looked at her sharply.

'You're such a good-looking girl, I expect all the gentlemen give you a lot of attention. Gentlemen are all very much alike in some ways – even if they are quite *old*...'

'You are extraordinary!' said Lucy. 'How do you know these things? But I don't think it's my good looks – they must think I know something.' She laughed.

But Inspector Craddock did not laugh. 'Be careful. They might murder you instead of asking you to marry them.'

Lucy was suddenly serious. 'I keep forgetting what happened. The boys have been having such fun that I began to think of it all as a game. But it's not a game.'

'No,' said Miss Marple. 'Murder isn't a game.' She paused. 'Will the boys go back to school soon?'

'Yes, next week. Tomorrow they go to James's home for the last few days of the holidays.'

'I'm glad of that,' said Miss Marple. 'I would not like anything to happen while they are at Rutherford Hall.'

Craddock looked at her thoughtfully. 'You don't believe that an unknown woman was murdered by an unknown man? You think that the crime was connected to Rutherford Hall?'

'I think there's a definite connection, yes.'

'All we know about the murderer is that he's a tall dark-haired man. On the day of the inquest, when I came out, the three brothers were standing waiting for the car. I could only see their backs, not their faces, and it was remarkable how, in their heavy coats, they looked all alike. *Three tall, dark-haired men.* And yet, actually, they're all quite different. It makes it very difficult.'

'I wonder,' said Miss Marple. 'Whether it might perhaps be all much *simpler* than we think. Murders so often are simple – with an obvious unpleasant motive...'

'If Martine exists,' said Craddock, 'there *is* a motive. If she appeared again with a son it would make the amount each Crackenthorpe inherited smaller – they're all very short of money.'

'Even Harold?' asked Lucy.

'He's been involved in some rather risky deals. A large sum of money, soon, might save him.'

'But if so...' said Lucy, and stopped.

'I know, dear,' said Miss Marple. 'It's the wrong murder, that's what you mean.'

'Yes. Martine's death wouldn't help Harold – or any of the others. Not until...'

'Not until Luther Crackenthorpe died. Exactly.'

'And he'll go on for years,' said Lucy. 'Although he was rather ill at Christmas-time. He said the doctor made a lot of fuss about it – "Anyone would think I'd been poisoned by the fuss he made." That's what he said.'

'Yes,' said Craddock. 'I want to ask Dr Quimper about that.'

CHAPTER 17

The doctor looked very tired that evening as he offered Craddock a drink and poured one for himself as well. 'Well, how can I help you?'

'First, thank you for advising Miss Crackenthorpe to come to me with the letter that said it was from her brother's widow.'

'Oh, I didn't exactly advise her to come. She wanted to.'

'Do you think it really was from Martine?'

'I don't know. I never saw it, but I think it was probably from someone who knew the facts and was trying to get some money from the family.' He paused. 'But why ask *me*? I've got nothing to do with it?'

'I really came to ask you something else…'

Dr Quimper looked interested.

'I have heard that at Christmas Mr Crackenthorpe was suddenly rather ill with a stomach upset.'

'Yes.'

'Mr Crackenthorpe mentioned you. I'm sorry, Doctor – he said you made a silly fuss about it.'

Quimper smiled. 'He said you had asked him lots of questions, not only about what he had eaten, but about who prepared it and served it.'

The doctor was not smiling now. 'Go on.'

'He said you talked as though you believed someone had poisoned him. Did you believe that?'

Quimper said, 'Do you think a doctor can suggest that someone has been poisoned without any proof?'

'I'd just like to know if you suspected he had been poisoned.'

Dr Quimper said, 'Old Crackenthorpe usually eats very little. When the family comes down, Emma increases the amount of food. Result – gastro-enteritis.'

'So you were not at all – puzzled?'

'All right. Yes, I was puzzled! Does that please you?'

'It interests me,' said Craddock. 'Why were you puzzled?'

'Because there were certain signs that were more like arsenic poisoning than ordinary gastro-enteritis. Although the two things are very much alike.'

'And what was the result of your inquiries?'

'That what I suspected could not possibly be true. Mr Crackenthorpe told me that he had had similar upsets before I had been his doctor, and always when he had eaten too much rich food.'

'Which was when the house was full? With the family? Or guests?'

'Yes. So I wrote to Dr Morris. He was my older partner who stopped working soon after I joined him. I asked about the earlier upsets that Mr Crackenthorpe had had.'

'And what did he say?'

Quimper smiled. 'He told me not to be so silly.'

'I wonder. Crackenthorpe is a healthy old man, do you think he might live to be ninety?'

'Easily.'

'And his sons – and daughter – are all getting older too, and they all need money?'

'You leave Emma out of it. She's no poisoner. These upsets only happen when the others are there – not when she and he are alone.'

'Very wise of her if she was the poisoner,' the Inspector thought, but did not say so. He paused. 'But suppose arsenic *was* put in his food, hasn't Crackenthorpe been very lucky not to die?'

'Well yes,' said the doctor. 'It's obviously not a case of small amounts of arsenic given regularly – which is the usual method of arsenic poisoning. So if these upsets are not from natural causes, it looks as though the poisoner is getting it wrong every time. Why hasn't he increased the amount? It doesn't make sense.'

'I agree,' the Inspector said. 'It doesn't seem to make sense.'

II

'Inspector Craddock!'

The excited whisper made him jump. Craddock had just been going to ring the front-door bell when Alexander and Stoddart-West appeared from the shadows.

'We've found a clue,' Alexander said. 'Come with us.'

A little <u>unwillingly</u>, he followed them round the corner of Rutherford Hall and into a yard where Stoddart-West pushed open a heavy door.

'It really *is* a clue, sir,' said Stoddart-West, his eyes shining behind his glasses. 'We found it this afternoon.'

'You see that big rubbish bin?' said Alexander. 'Hillman keeps it full of waste paper for when the <u>boiler</u> goes out and he wants to start it again.'

'Any odd paper that's blowing about. He picks it up and puts it in there...'

'And that's where we found it—'

'Found WHAT?' Craddock interrupted.

'*The clue.* Show him, James.'

Stoddart-West took from his pocket an envelope which he handed to the Inspector.

The clue had been through the post, there was no letter inside, it was just a torn envelope – addressed to Mrs Martine Crackenthorpe, 126 Elvers Crescent, N10.

'You see?' said Alexander. 'It shows she *was* here – Uncle Edmund's French wife...'

Stoddart-West interrupted. 'Don't you think, sir, that it *must* have been her in the sarcophagus?'

'You'll test it for <u>fingerprints</u>, won't you, sir?'

'Of course,' said Craddock.

'Good luck for us, wasn't it?' Stoddart-West said. 'On our last day, too.'

'I'm going to James's place tomorrow,' said Alexander. 'His parents have got a beautiful house – built in the time of Queen Anne, wasn't it?'

'William and Mary.'

'I thought your mother said...'

'Mum's French,' said Stoddart-West. 'She doesn't really know about English houses.'

Craddock was examining the envelope. How clever of Lucy Eyelesbarrow to put a post mark on it. Great fun for the boys. 'Come on,' he said, 'You've been very helpful.'

CHAPTER 18

The boys led Craddock through the back door into the house. In the kitchen Lucy was rolling out <u>pastry</u>. Leaning against the wall was Bryan Eastley.

'Hello, Dad,' said Alexander kindly. 'You out here again?'

'I like it out here,' said Bryan. 'Have you come to inspect the kitchen, Inspector?'

'Not exactly. I'd like to speak to Mr Cedric Crackenthorpe.'

'I'll go and see if he's in,' said Bryan and left the room.

'Is it nearly supper-time?' asked Alexander.

'No,' said Lucy. 'There's some chocolate cake in the food cupboard.'

The boys rushed together out of the door.

'You are very clever,' said Craddock.

'Why?'

'Because of how you did this!' He showed her the envelope.

'What *are* you talking about?' She looked at him.

Craddock suddenly felt a bit faint. 'Didn't you put this in the bin, for the boys to find?'

'What! Do you mean that…?'

Craddock put the envelope quickly back in his pocket as Bryan returned.

'Cedric's in the library.'

II

Cedric seemed delighted to see the Inspector. 'So have you found out who the dead woman was?'

'We have a good idea. But we want to get some statements. I would like you to tell me exactly what you were doing on Friday 20th December.'

Cedric leaned back. 'Well, as I've already told you, I was in Ibiza, and one day there is so like another. Painting in the morning, sleep in the afternoon. After that some kind of a meal. Most of the evening in Scotty's Bar with friends. Will that do?'

'I'd rather have the truth, Mr Crackenthorpe.'

Cedric sat up. 'That's a most offensive remark, Inspector.'

'Really? You told me that you left Ibiza on 21st December and arrived in England that same day?'

'Yes, I did.'

'You must think we are very stupid,' said Craddock pleasantly. 'If you'll show me your passport—'

'I can't find it,' said Cedric.

'I think you could find it, but it's not really necessary because the records show that you entered this country on the evening of 19th December. Perhaps you will now tell me what you did between that time until lunch-time on 21st December when you arrived here.'

Cedric looked very angry. 'You can't do anything you want to any more! Somebody's always asking questions. And what's special about the 20th?'

'It's the day we believe the murder was committed.'

'Well, yes,' Cedric said. 'I left Ibiza on the 19th. There was a very attractive woman on the plane... we got to London and stayed at the Kingsway Palace, in case your spies haven't found that out yet! I called myself John Brown.'

'And on the 20th?'

'I stayed in bed all morning, as I'd had rather a lot to drink.'

'And the afternoon?'

'I went into the National Gallery. Then I saw a film. Then I had a drink or two in the bar, and at about ten o'clock I went out with the girlfriend to various nightclubs – can't remember much more till I woke up the next morning – when the girlfriend ran off to catch her plane to America and I poured cold water over my head, and then left for this place.'

'Can any of this be proved, Mr Crackenthorpe? Say between 3 pm and 7 pm.'

'Most unlikely,' said Cedric cheerfully.

The door opened and Emma entered the room with a diary in her hand. 'I believe you want to know what everyone was doing on 20th December, Inspector Craddock?'

'Er – yes, Miss Crackenthorpe.'

'Well, I went into Brackhampton for a church meeting. That finished about a quarter to one and I lunched with Lady Adington and Miss Bartlett at the Cadena Café. After lunch I did some Christmas shopping. I had tea at about a quarter to five in the Shamrock Tea Rooms and then went to the station to meet Bryan.'

'Thank you, Miss Crackenthorpe, that is very helpful.' Craddock did not tell her that as she was a woman, height five foot seven, her movements were not important. Instead he said, 'Your other two brothers came down later?'

'Alfred came down late on Saturday evening. He says he tried to phone me that afternoon but I was out. Harold did not come down until Christmas Eve.'

Craddock took the envelope from his pocket. 'Do you recognize this?'

'But…' Emma looked at him, shocked. 'That's the letter I wrote to Martine. Did she…? Have you found her?'

'It is possible that we have – found her. This empty envelope was found *here*.'

'Then – it was Martine – in the sarcophagus?'

'It seems very likely,' said Craddock gently.

It seemed even more likely when he got back to town and found a message from Armand Dessin.

> One of her friends has had a postcard from Anna Stravinska. The holiday story was true! She has reached Jamaica and is having a wonderful time!

Craddock <u>crushed</u> the message and threw it into the rubbish bin.

CHAPTER 19

'Not very helpful,' said Sergeant Wetherall.

Craddock was reading through the report on Harold Crackenthorpe's alibi for 20th December.

He had been noticed at Sotheby's at about three-thirty, but had left soon after that. His photograph had not been recognized at Russell's tea-shop, but his <u>manservant</u> said that he had returned to Cardigan Gardens to dress for his dinner party at a quarter to seven – rather late, since the dinner was at seven-thirty. He did not remember hearing him come in that evening, but he often did not hear him. The garage where Harold kept his car was rented and so no one noticed who came and went there.

'He was at the Catering Club Dinner, but left before the end of the speeches,' said Wetherall.

Craddock stretched out his hand for the information on Cedric. That also was negative, though a taxi driver said he might have taken him to Paddington station that afternoon. 'Dirty trousers and untidy hair. He <u>swore</u> a bit because fares had gone up since he was last in England.'

'And here's Alfred,' said the Sergeant.

Something in his voice made Craddock look up. Wetherall had the pleased look of a man who has kept the best news until the end.

The check was mainly negative. Alfred came and went at different times. Most of his neighbours were out at work all day. But towards the end of the report, Wetherall's large finger pointed to the final words.

Sergeant Leakie, who had been working on cases of things stolen from lorries, had been at a café on the Waddington–Brackhampton Road, watching certain lorry drivers. He had noticed at a nearby table, Chick Evans, one of Dicky Rogers' friends. With him had been Alfred Crackenthorpe. Time, 9.30 pm, Friday 20th December.

Alfred Crackenthorpe had got on a bus a few minutes later, going in the direction of Brackhampton. William Baker, ticket collector at Brackhampton, had checked the ticket of a gentleman whom he recognized as one of Miss Crackenthorpe's brothers, just before the 11.55 train left for Paddington. He remembered the day because there had been a story of some mad old lady who said she had seen somebody murdered in a train that afternoon.

'It puts him right at the exact place, there,' Wetherall said.

Craddock nodded. Yes, Alfred could have travelled down by the 4.33 to Brackhampton, committing murder on the way. Then he could have gone out by bus to the café. He could have left there at nine-thirty and would have had plenty of time to go to Rutherford Hall, move the body from the embankment to the sarcophagus, and get into Brackhampton in time to catch the 11.55 back to London.

II

At Rutherford Hall there had been a gathering of the Crackenthorpe family and very soon voices were raised.

Lucy decided to mix some cocktails in a jug and then took them towards the library. The voices sounded clearly in the hall.

Dr Quimper came out of the study where he had been with Mr Crackenthorpe. He saw the jug in Lucy's hand. 'What's this? A celebration?'

'More like a calming medicine. They're having a big argument in there.'

'Blaming each other?'

'Mostly Emma.'

'Are they?' Dr Quimper took the jug from Lucy's hand, opened the library door and went in. 'Good evening.'

'Ah, Dr Quimper,' Harold said. 'I would like to know why you involved yourself in a family matter, and told my sister to go to Scotland Yard about it.'

Dr Quimper said calmly, 'Miss Crackenthorpe asked my advice. I gave it to her.'

'You dare to…'

'Girl!' Mr Crackenthorpe looked out of the study door just behind Lucy. 'I want curry for dinner tonight. You make a very good curry. It's ages since we've had curry.'

'All right, Mr Crackenthorpe.'

Lucy went back to the kitchen and began to peel some mushrooms. The front door banged and from the window she saw Dr Quimper walk angrily to his car and drive away.

III

It was 3 am when Dr Quimper drove his car into his garage. Well, Mrs Josh Simpkins now had a healthy baby. He went upstairs to his bedroom. He was tired – very tired. He looked with pleasure at his bed. Then the telephone rang.

'Dr Quimper?'

'Yes.'

'This is Lucy Eyelesbarrow from Rutherford Hall. Please can you come over. Everybody here suddenly has an upset stomach.'

'I'll be over immediately.' He hurried down to his car again.

IV

It was three hours later when the doctor and Lucy sat down at the kitchen table to drink large cups of black coffee.

'Well, I think they'll be all right now,' he said. 'But how did it happen? That's what I want to know. What did they have for dinner?'

'Mushroom soup. Curried chicken and rice. Fruit jelly.'

'All right – so most people would say, "It must have been the mushrooms".'

'It wasn't the mushrooms. I had some of the soup myself and I'm all right.'

'Yes, *you're* all right.'

'If you mean…'

'No. You're a clever girl. You would be pretending to be ill, too, if you had put poison in the food. Anyway, I know all about you. I made some inquiries. And you're not a girlfriend of either Cedric, Harold or Alfred – helping them to do unpleasant things.'

'Do you really think…?'

'I think quite a lot of things,' said Quimper. 'But I have to be careful what I say. Now, curried chicken. Did you have some of that?'

'No. When you've cooked a curry, the smell makes you feel you've already eaten it. I tasted it, of course. And I had some jelly.'

'How did you serve the jelly?'

'In separate glasses.'

'And how much of all this has been washed up?'

'Everything.'

'A pity,' Dr Quimper said. 'Is there any of the food left?'

'There's some of the curry, and some soup. No jelly.'

'I'll take the curry and the soup.' He stood up. 'And if you can manage until the morning, I'll send a nurse here by eight o'clock.' Dr Quimper put a hand on her shoulder. 'Look after two people in particular. Emma – well, Emma means a lot to me. And look after the old man. I can't say that he's ever been my favourite patient, but he *is* my patient, and I'm not going to let him be rushed out of the world because one of his unpleasant sons wants his money.'

V

Inspector Bacon was looking upset. 'Arsenic?' he said. 'Arsenic?'

'Yes. It was in the curry.'

'So there's a poisoner at work?'

'It seems so,' said Dr Quimper.

'And they've all been ill, you say – except that Miss Eyelesbarrow. That's a bit strange...'

'If Miss Eyelesbarrow was feeding the family arsenic, she would be careful to eat a very small amount of the poisoned curry, and then behave as though she was very ill.'

'And you wouldn't be able to tell that she'd had less than the others?'

'Probably not.'

'Then there might be one of the family now who's making more fuss than he need?'

'Yes. But I don't think that anyone has had enough arsenic to kill them.'

'Did the poisoner make a mistake?'

'No. I think that the idea was to put enough arsenic in the curry to cause signs of food poisoning – which everyone would say was because of the mushrooms. Then one person would probably suddenly get worse and die.'

'Because he had been given more poison?'

The doctor nodded. 'So, perhaps you can go to Rutherford Hall and tell them all that they're suffering from arsenic poisoning. That will probably stop the poisoner carrying out the rest of his plan.'

The telephone rang on the Inspector's desk. He picked it up. 'OK. Yes.' He said to Quimper, 'It's your nurse.' He handed it to him.

'Quimper speaking... I see... Yes, we'll be with you very soon.' He put the telephone down and turned to Bacon. 'It's Alfred. He's dead.'

CHAPTER 20

'Alfred?' Craddock said over the phone. *'Alfred?'*

Inspector Bacon said, 'You didn't expect that?'

'No, not at all. In fact I thought he was the murderer!' There was a moment's silence. Then he asked, 'There was a nurse in charge. How did she allow it to happen?'

'We can't blame her. Miss Eyelesbarrow was very tired and went to bed for a bit. The nurse had five patients to look after, and old Mr Crackenthorpe started making a big fuss, so she had to go and help him and then took Alfred in some tea. He drank it and that was the end.'

'Arsenic again?'

'It seems so.'

'I wonder,' said Craddock, 'whether Alfred was *meant* to be the victim?'

'You mean the tea *might* have been meant for the old man.'

'Are they sure that the arsenic was in the tea?'

'No. The nurse washed the cups and everything. But it seems the only likely method.'

'So,' said Craddock, 'one of the patients wasn't as ill as the others? Saw his chance and poisoned the cup?'

'Well, there won't be any more of that,' said Inspector Bacon. 'I've got two men there. Are you coming down?'

'As fast as I can!'

II

Lucy Eyelesbarrow came across the hall to meet the Inspector. She looked pale.

'You've been having a bad time,' said Craddock.

'It's been like a bad dream.'

'About this curry—'

'It was the curry?'

'Yes, arsenic was found in it.'

'Then it must be one of the family who did it.'

'There is no other possibility?'

'No, you see, I only started making the curry late – after six o'clock – because Mr Crackenthorpe specially asked for curry.'

'Which of them had the chance to do something to the curry while it was cooking?'

Lucy thought. 'Anyone could have come into the kitchen while I was laying the table in the dining room.'

'So who was here in the house? Mr Crackenthorpe, Emma, Cedric…'

'Harold and Alfred. Oh, and Bryan Eastley. But he left just before dinner.'

'Well, look after yourself,' said Craddock. 'There's a poisoner in this house, remember, and one of your patients probably isn't as ill as he pretends to be.'

Lucy went upstairs again after Craddock had gone and as she passed Mr Crackenthorpe's room she heard him calling, 'Girl – girl – come here.'

Lucy entered the room.

Mr Crackenthorpe was sitting up in bed looking very cheerful. 'So Alfred won't get any of the money. They've all been waiting for *me* to die – Alfred in particular. Now he's dead. That's rather a good joke.' He laughed. 'I'll live longer than them all.'

CHAPTER 21

Lucy was busy arranging trays to take to the various sick people. She picked up the first one and took it upstairs.

'What's *this*?' said Mr Crackenthorpe.

'Tea and rice pudding,' said Lucy.

'Take it away. I told that nurse I wanted meat. What's Emma doing? Why doesn't she come and see me?'

'She's still in bed, Mr Crackenthorpe.'

'Women are so weak. But you're a good strong girl. And I've got a nice store of money and I know who I'm going to spend it on when the time comes.' He smiled and tried to hold her hand.

Lucy went rather quickly out of the room.

The next tray she took in to Emma.

'Oh, thank you, Lucy. But I'm worried about your aunt,' she said as Lucy put the tray on her knees. 'You haven't had any time to go and see her.'

'Oh, don't worry. She understands how difficult things have been.'

But as she went down to fetch the next tray, Lucy decided that she would ring Miss Marple up as soon as she had taken Cedric his meal.

Cedric was sitting up in bed, writing. 'Hello, Lucy, what awful food have you got for me today? I wish you would get rid of that nurse. She calls me "we" for some reason. "And how are we this morning? Have we slept well?"'

'You seem very cheerful,' said Lucy. 'And busy. What are you writing?'

'Plans for what to do with this place when the old man dies. If I sell all the land, I'll have more money than I know what to do with.'

'I thought you disliked money.'

'Of course I dislike money when I haven't got any,' said Cedric. 'What a lovely girl you are, Lucy, or do I just think so because I haven't seen any good-looking women for such a long time?'

'I expect that's it,' said Lucy.

Before getting her own lunch she went to the telephone and rang up Miss Marple. 'I'm very sorry I haven't been able to come over, but I've been so busy.'

'Of course, my dear, but there's nothing that can be done just now. And Elspeth McGillicuddy will be home very soon. I wrote to her to come at once.'

'You don't think…' Lucy stopped.

'That there will be any more deaths? Oh, I hope not. But one never knows, does one? When someone is really evil, I mean.'

Lucy rang off and took her tray into the small study. She was just finishing her meal when the door opened and Bryan Eastley came in.

'Hello,' she said. 'This is very unexpected.'

'I suppose it is,' said Bryan. 'How is everybody?'

'Oh, much better. Harold's going back to London tomorrow. Have you come to stay?'

'Well, I'd like to, if it won't be too much work for you.'

'No, we can manage,' said Lucy, picking up the tray.

'I'll do that,' said Bryan, taking it from her. They went into the kitchen together. 'Shall I help you wash up? I do like this kitchen. In fact I like this whole house.' He picked up a cloth and began to wipe the spoons and forks. 'It seems a waste, it all going to Cedric. He'll just sell it and go abroad again. Harold wouldn't want this house either, and of course it's much too big for Emma. But if it came to Alexander, he and I would be as happy together here as two children. But before Alexander could get this place all of them would have to die, and that's not likely, is it?'

CHAPTER 22

The next day when Lucy heard the door bell ring, she went to answer it, expecting to see the doctor. But it was not the doctor. At the door stood a tall, stylish woman. In the drive was a Rolls Royce.

'Can I see Miss Emma Crackenthorpe, please?' It was a pleasant voice, French perhaps.

'I'm sorry, Miss Crackenthorpe is ill and can't see anyone.'

'I know she has been ill, yes; but it is very important that I see her. You are Miss Eyelesbarrow, I think. My son has told me about you. I am Lady Stoddart-West.'

'Oh, I see,' said Lucy.

Lady Stoddart-West continued, 'I need to speak to Emma because of something that the boys have said to me. Please, will you ask her?'

'Come in.' Lucy took her visitor into the sitting room, then she went upstairs, knocked on Emma's door. 'Lady Stoddart-West is here. She wants to see you about something the boys have told her.'

'Oh. Well… perhaps I ought to see her.'

Lucy led the visitor upstairs, opened the bedroom door for her to go in and then shut it.

Lady Stoddart-West moved across the room. 'Miss Crackenthorpe? We have met before, I think, at the sports day at the school.'

'Yes,' said Emma, 'Please sit down.'

Lady Stoddart-West sat in a chair beside the bed. 'You must think it very strange of me to come like this, but the boys have been very excited about the murder that happened here.'

Emma said, 'You think we ought to have sent your son home earlier?'

'No, no, that is not what I think. Oh, this is difficult for me! But the boys told me that the police think that the murdered woman may be a French girl whom your eldest brother knew during the war. Is that right?'

'It is possible,' said Emma.

'But why do they think that she is Martine? Did she have letters with her?'

'No. But you see, I had a letter, from this Martine.'

'You had a letter – from *Martine*?'

'Yes, saying she would like to come and see me. I invited her here, but got a message saying she was going back to France. But then an envelope was found here addressed to her, so…'

Lady Stoddart-West said quickly, 'When I heard this, I had to come and tell you something that I never intended to tell you. You see, *I am Martine Dubois*.'

Emma stared at her. 'You! You are Martine?'

'But, yes. I met your brother Edmund in the first days of the war. He was staying at our house. We fell in love. We intended to be married, and then Edmund was killed. I will not speak to you of that time. But I will say to you that I loved your brother very much… Then the Germans occupied France and I helped Englishmen get from France to England. That was how I met my present husband. He was an Air Force officer. When the war was over I had a new life and did not want to think about the past.' She paused. 'But it gave me a strange pleasure when I found out that my son's best friend at his school was Edmund's nephew.'

'I can hardly believe it,' said Emma, 'that *you* are the Martine that dear Edmund told me about. But was it you, then, who wrote to me?'

Lady Stoddart-West shook her head. 'No, no, of course I did not write to you.'

'Then...' Emma stopped.

'Then there was someone pretending to be Martine, who wanted perhaps to get money from you? But who can it be? I have never said anything about it since I came to England.'

Emma said, 'We will have to tell Inspector Craddock.' She looked with suddenly gentle eyes at her visitor. 'I'm so glad to know you at last, my dear.'

'And I you.'

Emma leaned back. 'Thank goodness, I don't know who the poor woman was, but if she wasn't Martine, then she can't be connected to *us*!'

CHAPTER 23

The neat secretary brought Harold Crackenthorpe his usual afternoon cup of tea.

'Thanks, Miss Ellis, I shall be going home early today.'

'I don't really think you should have come in at all, Mr Crackenthorpe. You don't look well.'

'I'm all right,' said Harold, but he did not feel well.

He shouldn't really have come into the office, but he had wanted to see how the business was going. All this – he looked round him – appeared successful. But now it wouldn't be long before his business failed. If only his father had died instead of Alfred, there wouldn't have been anything to worry about.

But with Alfred gone, the money from his grandfather would be divided not into five shares but into four. Looking more cheerful, Harold got up, left the office and drove home.

Darwin, his servant, opened the door. 'Her ladyship has just arrived, sir.'

For a moment Harold stared at him. Alice! Was it really today that Alice was coming back from the Riviera? He had forgotten all about it.

He had never been in love with her, of course, but her rich family had been useful. Though not perhaps as useful as they might have been, because he and Alice had never had any children.

He went upstairs into the sitting room. 'My dear, how was San Raphael?'

Alice told him how San Raphael was. She was a thin woman with sandy-coloured hair, and pale grey eyes. She also asked about her husband's health. 'Emma's telegram rather frightened me. I read in the paper the other day of forty people in a hotel getting food poisoning. All these <u>refrigerators</u> are dangerous. People keep things in them too long and forget about them.'

'Possibly,' said Harold.

'Oh, and I nearly forgot to tell you there's a parcel for you on the hall table.'

'Is there? I didn't notice it.' Harold went and picked up the parcel, which was small and very carefully wrapped. He took it back into the sitting room where he opened it. Inside was a small pill box with *Two to be taken each night* written on it. With it was a small piece of paper from the chemist's in Brackhampton with *Sent by request of Doctor Quimper* written on it.

'What is it, dear?' said Alice. 'You look worried.'

'Oh, it's just – some pills. But I'm sure the doctor said I need not take any more.'

His wife said calmly, 'He probably said don't forget to take them.'

'Perhaps he did.' Harold looked across at her and for a moment he wondered exactly what she was thinking. That calm expression told him nothing. Her eyes were like windows in an empty house. What did Alice feel about him? Had she ever been in love with him?

'I think I shall go to bed,' he said. 'It's been my first day back in the City.'

'Yes, I think that's a good idea. And don't forget to take your pills, dear.'

He went upstairs. Yes, it would be wrong to stop taking the pills so soon. He took two and swallowed them with a glass of water.

CHAPTER 24

'Nobody could possibly have made more mistakes than I have.' Dermot Craddock sat in Florence's sitting room looking tired and upset. 'I've let a whole family be poisoned. Alfred Crackenthorpe's dead and now Harold's dead too. What going on here?'

'Poisoned pills,' said Miss Marple thoughtfully.

'Yes. Very clever. They looked just like the pills that he had been taking. But Quimper never ordered them. And the chemist knew nothing about them, either. No. That box of pills came from Rutherford Hall.'

'Do you *know* it came from Rutherford Hall?'

'Yes. It's the box that held Emma's sleeping pills.'

'Oh, I see. Emma's…'

'Yes. It's got her fingerprints on it and the fingerprints of both the nurses and the fingerprints of the chemist. Nobody else's, of course.'

'And the sleeping pills were removed and something else put in the box?'

'Yes.'

'What were the pills Harold took?' Miss Marple asked.

'Aconite. They are usually kept in a poison bottle. I don't know who poisoned Harold, I don't know who poisoned Alfred, and now the real Martine turns out to be the wife of Sir Robert Stoddart-West! So, who's the woman in the barn? I don't know. At first I was sure it was Anna Stravinska, but then *she's* out of it—'

Miss Marple gave a small cough. 'But is she?'

'Well, that postcard from Jamaica…'

'Yes,' said Miss Marple, 'but anyone can get a postcard sent from almost anywhere, don't you think?'

'Yes,' said Craddock. 'And of course we would have checked that postcard if it hadn't been for the Martine business fitting in so well. The envelope of the letter Emma wrote to her was even found at Rutherford Hall, showing she had actually been there.'

'But the murdered woman *hadn't* been there!' Miss Marple said. 'Not in the sense *you* mean. *She* only came to Rutherford Hall *after she was dead.*'

'Oh, yes.'

'What the envelope really proves is that the *murderer* was there. Presumably he took that envelope off her with her other things, and then dropped it by mistake – or – I wonder, was it a mistake? Your men must have searched the place, but they didn't find it. It only turned up later in the bin.'

'You think the boys were meant to find it?'

'Well, it stopped you thinking about Anna Stravinska any more, didn't it?'

'But the main fact is that someone was going to pretend to be Martine,' said Craddock. 'And then for some reason – didn't. Why?'

'That's a very interesting question,' said Miss Marple.

'Somebody sent a note saying Martine was going back to France, then arranged to travel down with the girl and kill her on the way. You agree?'

'Not exactly,' said Miss Marple. 'I don't think, really, you're making it simple enough.'

'Simple! So do you or do you not think you know who the murdered woman was?'

'It's so difficult to explain,' Miss Marple said. 'I mean, I don't know *who* she was, but I'm sure who she *was*, if you know what I mean.'

'Know what you mean?' Craddock shook his head. 'I haven't any idea.' He looked out through the window. 'There's Lucy Eyelesbarrow coming to see you, so I'll go. My confidence is very low this afternoon and meeting such a clever young woman is too much for me.'

'I suppose it was always sure to cause trouble,' said Lucy, walking up and down the room. 'A will leaving money to several people, but saying that if, when the time came for it to be handed out, there was only one person left, he would get the lot. And yet – there was such a lot of money, you would think it would be enough...'

'The trouble is,' said Miss Marple, 'that people always want more money. Some people. They don't start with wanting to commit murder, they just start by wanting more than they're going to have.'

'But we've now had three murders and that only leaves two to inherit the money, doesn't it?'

'You mean Cedric and Emma,' said Miss Marple.

'Not Emma. Emma isn't a tall dark-haired man. No. I mean Cedric and Bryan Eastley. I never thought of Bryan because he's fair, but the other day...' She paused.

'Go on,' said Miss Marple.

'It was when Lady Stoddart-West was leaving. She was getting into the car when she suddenly asked, "Who was that tall, dark-haired man who was standing on the lawn as I came in?"

'I didn't know who she meant at first, because Cedric was still in bed. So I said, "You don't mean Bryan Eastley?" and she said, "Of course, <u>Squadron Leader</u> Eastley. He was hidden in our house in France once during the war. I remembered the way he stood".'

Miss Marple said nothing.

'And then, later I looked at him... He was standing with his back to me and I saw that even when a man is fair, his hair can look dark if he smooths it down with cream. So you see, it might have been *Bryan* that your friend saw in the train. It might...'

'Yes,' said Miss Marple. 'I had thought of that.'

'But the money would go to Alexander, not to him.'

'If anything happened to Alexander before he was twenty-one, then Bryan would get the money,' Miss Marple said.

Lucy looked shocked. 'He would never do *that*. No father would ever do that.'

Miss Marple shook her head. 'People do, my dear. It's very sad and very awful, but they do.' She added gently, 'But you mustn't worry. Elspeth McGillicuddy will be here very soon now.'

'I don't see how that will help.'

'No, dear, perhaps not. But *I* think it's important.' Then, with a quick look at Lucy, she said, 'There's something else that's worrying you.'

'Yes. Something that I didn't understand until two days ago. Bryan could in fact have been on that train.'

'On the 4.33 from Paddington?'

'Yes. You see, Emma, when talking about *her* movements on 20th December, said *she went to meet Bryan at the station*. The train she met was the 4.50 from Paddington, but he could have been on the earlier train and pretended to come on the later one. It doesn't really prove anything. The awful thing is not *knowing* what happened. And perhaps we never will know!'

'Of course we will know, dear,' said Miss Marple. 'The one thing I *do* know about murderers is that they can never leave things alone. Particularly after they've committed a second murder. And the great thing is that Elspeth McGillicuddy will be here very soon now!'

CHAPTER 26

'Now, Elspeth, you do know what I want you to do?'

'Yes, I know,' said Mrs McGillicuddy, 'but what I say to you is, Jane, that it seems very strange.'

'It's not strange at all,' said Miss Marple.

'To arrive at the house and to ask almost immediately whether I can – er – go upstairs?'

'It's very cold weather.'

'If you would just tell me why I must go upstairs, Jane.'

'That's just what I don't want to do,' said Miss Marple.

'How annoying you are. First you make me come all the way back to England before…'

'I'm sorry about that, but someone may soon be killed. So you see, Elspeth, it was your duty to come back. And that's the taxi now,' she added, as a sound was heard outside the house.

So Mrs McGillicuddy put on her coat and the two ladies were driven to Rutherford Hall.

II

'Who can this be?' Emma asked, looking out of the window, as the taxi moved past it. 'I do believe it's Lucy's old aunt.'

'What a bore,' said Cedric. 'Tell her you're not at home.'

But at that moment the door was opened by Mrs Hart, who was there that afternoon to clean the silver, and Miss Marple came in, with another woman behind her.

'I do hope,' said Miss Marple, taking Emma's hand, 'that this is not inconvenient. But I'm going home the day after tomorrow, and so I wanted to say goodbye… Oh, may I introduce my friend, Mrs McGillicuddy, who is visiting?'

At this moment Lucy entered the room. 'Aunt Jane, I had no idea…'

'I had to come and thank Miss Crackenthorpe,' said Miss Marple, 'who has been so very, very kind to you, Lucy.'

'It's Lucy who's been very kind to us,' said Emma.

'Oh, yes,' said Cedric. 'We've certainly made her work for her money. Looking after us when we were ill, running up and down the stairs…'

Miss Marple interrupted. 'So dangerous, isn't it, food poisoning? Mushrooms, I heard.'

'The cause remains rather mysterious,' said Emma.

'Nonsense,' said Cedric, 'Arsenic in the curry, that's what it was. Lucy's aunt knows all about it, I'm sure.'

'Well,' said Miss Marple, 'I did just hear…'

The door opened and Mr Crackenthorpe came in. 'Where's tea? You! Girl! Why haven't you brought tea in?'

'It's just ready, Mr Crackenthorpe.'

Lucy went out of the room then reappeared with a tea tray. Bryan Eastley followed her, carrying sandwiches and cake.

'What's this? What's this?' Mr Crackenthorpe asked. 'A decorated cake? Are we having a party? Nobody told me about it.'

Emma's face went pink. 'Dr Quimper's coming to tea, Father. It's his birthday today and…'

'Birthday? Birthdays are only for children. I won't let anyone celebrate my birthdays.'

'Emma, what a delightful view you have from this window,' said Miss Marple, moving across to it. 'Just like a picture with the cows there under the trees. I can't believe that I am in the middle of a town.'

'If the windows were open, you would hear far off the noise of the traffic,' said Emma.

'Oh, of course,' said Miss Marple, 'there's noise everywhere, isn't there? Even in St Mary Mead. Really, the way those jet planes fly over! Two windows in my little <u>greenhouse</u> were broken the other day. I can't understand why.'

'It's quite simple, really,' said Bryan, coming to the window.

Miss Marple dropped her handbag and Bryan politely picked it up. At the same moment Mrs McGillicuddy said to Emma, 'I wonder – could I go upstairs for a moment?'

'I'll take you,' said Lucy, and they left the room together.

'It is very cold outside today,' said Miss Marple.

'About planes breaking windows,' said Bryan. 'Oh, look, there's Quimper.'

The doctor drove up in his car. He came in, rubbing his hands. 'It's going to snow, I think. Hello, Emma, how are you? Goodness, what's all this?'

'You told me today was your birthday,' said Emma. 'So we made you a cake.'

'But it's years since anyone's remembered my birthday.' He looked almost uncomfortably pleased.

'Come on, let's have tea,' said Mr Crackenthorpe. 'What are we waiting for?'

'Oh, please,' said Miss Marple, 'don't wait for my friend. She would be most upset if you did.'

They sat down and started tea. Miss Marple reached for a sandwich, then paused. 'Are they—?'

'Fish,' said Bryan. 'I helped make them.'

Mr Crackenthorpe laughed. 'Poisoned fish. That's what they are. You've got to be careful what you eat in this house, Miss Marple.'

'Don't let him stop you,' said Cedric. 'A bit of arsenic is good for the skin, they say, if you don't have too much.'

'Eat one yourself, boy,' said Mr Crackenthorpe.

'All right,' said Cedric. He took a sandwich and put it whole into his mouth.

Miss Marple also took a sandwich and bit into it. 'I do think it's so brave of you all to make these jokes.' Then suddenly she began to <u>choke</u>. 'A fish bone, in my throat.'

Quimper got up quickly. He went across to her, moved her backwards towards the window and told her to open her mouth. Then he looked down into the old lady's throat. At that moment the door opened and Mrs McGillicuddy, followed by Lucy, came in. Mrs McGillicuddy stopped as she saw the scene in front of her, Miss Marple leaning back and the doctor holding her throat.

'But that's *him*,' she cried. 'That's the man in the train...'

With unbelievable speed Miss Marple escaped from the doctor's hands and came towards her friend.

'I *thought* you'd recognize him, Elspeth! No. Don't say another word.' She turned to Dr Quimper. 'You didn't know, did you, Doctor, when you strangled that woman in the train, that somebody *actually saw you do it*? It was my friend here. She was in another train that was running parallel with yours.

'What?' Dr Quimper moved quickly towards Mrs McGillicuddy, but again, with unbelievable speed, Miss Marple was between them.

'Yes. She saw you, and *she recognizes you*, and she'll <u>swear</u> to it in court.'

'You disgusting old—' Dr Quimper stepped towards Miss Marple, but Cedric caught him by the shoulder.

'So *you're* the murderer. I never liked you, but I never suspected you.'

Bryan Eastley came quickly to help Cedric and at that moment Inspector Craddock and Inspector Bacon entered the room.

'Dr Quimper,' said Bacon, 'I must <u>caution</u> you that…'

'You can do what you like with your caution. Do you really think anyone's going to believe what a couple of old women say?' Dr Quimper suddenly laughed. 'Why should I want to murder a totally strange woman?'

'She wasn't a strange woman,' said Inspector Craddock. '*She was your wife.*'

CHAPTER 27

'So you see,' said Miss Marple, 'it really was very, very simple. So many men seem to murder their wives.'

Mrs McGillicuddy looked at Miss Marple and Inspector Craddock. 'Please explain it all to me.'

'He saw his chance, you see,' said Miss Marple, 'of having a rich wife, Emma Crackenthorpe. But he couldn't marry her because he had a wife already. They had been separated for years but she wouldn't divorce him. That fitted very well with what Inspector Craddock told me of a girl called Anna Stravinska. *She* had an English husband and she was a Catholic.

'So Dr Quimper decided to kill her. The idea of murdering her in the train and later putting her body in the sarcophagus was rather a clever one, because it would involve the Crackenthorpe family. Before that he had written a letter to Emma which said it was from Martine. Emma had told Dr Quimper all about her brother, you see. Then he encouraged her to go to the police with her story as he wanted the dead woman to be identified as Martine. I think he may have heard that inquiries were being made by the Paris police about Anna Stravinska, so he arranged to have a postcard come from her from Jamaica.

'It was easy for him to meet his wife in London, to tell her that he hoped they could be together again and that he would like her to come and "meet his family". We won't talk about the next part of it, which is very unpleasant. Of course all he wanted was money, so perhaps he had already thought about murdering the brothers before he decided to murder his wife. Anyway, he started the idea that someone was trying to poison old Mr Crackenthorpe, to prepare for his other crimes. And then he gave arsenic to the whole family. Not too much, of course, because he didn't want old Mr Crackenthorpe to die.'

'But I still don't see how he did that,' said Craddock. 'He wasn't in the house when the curry was being prepared.'

'Oh, but there wasn't any arsenic in the curry *then*,' said Miss Marple. 'He added it to the curry afterwards when he took it away to be tested. He probably put the arsenic in the cocktail jug earlier. Then, of course, it was easy for him, as a doctor, to poison Alfred Crackenthorpe and also to send the pills to Harold in London. Everything he did was planned and selfish and cruel.'

'I agree,' said Inspector Craddock.

'But I thought,' continued Miss Marple, 'that if Elspeth could see Dr Quimper in exactly the same position as she had seen him in the train, with his back to her, bent over a woman he was holding by the throat, then she would recognize him. That is why I had to prepare my little plan with Lucy's help.'

'I must say,' said Mrs McGillicuddy, 'it did give me a shock. I said, "That's him" before I could stop myself. Yet I hadn't in fact seen the man's *face* and...'

'I was afraid that you were going to say so, Elspeth,' said Miss Marple. 'And that would have been awful. Because he thought you really *did* recognize him. I mean, *he* couldn't know that you hadn't seen his face.'

'A good thing I said nothing then,' said Mrs McGillicuddy.

'I wasn't going to let you say another word,' said Miss Marple.

Craddock laughed. 'So, Miss Marple, what is the happy ending? What happens to poor Emma Crackenthorpe?'

'She'll soon forget the doctor, and perhaps go off on a holiday and meet someone else. A *nicer* man than Dr Quimper, I hope.'

'What about Lucy Eyelesbarrow? A wedding there, too?'

'Perhaps,' said Miss Marple.

'Which of all the men is she going to choose?' said Dermot Craddock.

'Don't you know?' said Miss Marple.

'No, I don't,' said Craddock. 'Do you?'

'Oh, yes, I think so,' said Miss Marple. And she smiled at him.

◆ CHARACTER LIST ◆

Mrs Elspeth McGillicuddy: a passenger on the 4.50 train from Paddington station

Miss Jane Marple: an elderly lady, a friend of Mrs McGillicuddy

Sergeant Frank Cornish: a police officer at St Mary Mead Police Station

David West: Miss Marple's nephew

Leonard Clement: son of the Vicar of St Mary Mead and his wife Griselda

Miss Florence Hill: former servant of Miss Marple

Miss Lucy Eyelesbarrow: a young professional house carer who is much cleverer than her job makes her seem

Miss Emma Crackenthorpe: Luther Crackenthorpe's middle-aged daughter

Mrs Kidder: a servant at Rutherford Hall

Mrs Hart: a servant at Rutherford Hall

Luther Crackenthorpe: elderly head of the family, owner of Rutherford Hall, Brackhampton

Cedric Crackenthorpe: Luther Crackenthorpe's eldest living son, an artist, who lives on Ibiza, an island in the Mediterranean

Harold Crackenthorpe: Luther Crackenthorpe's younger son, who works in finance in the City

Alfred Crackenthorpe: Luther Crackenthorpe's youngest son, who works at various things

Bryan Eastley: Luther Crackenthorpe's son-in-law, a widower (having married Edith Crackenthorpe, who died five years before) and former RAF pilot in the war

Alexander Eastley: Bryan Eastley's young son, and grandson of Luther Crackenthorpe

James Stoddart-West: a school friend of Alexander

Inspector Bacon: a senior police officer at Brackhampton Police

Dr Quimper: the Crackenthorpe family doctor

Mr Wimbourne: the Crackenthorpes' lawyer in London

Detective Inspector Dermot Craddock: the detective from Scotland Yard working on the murder case

Josiah Crackenthorpe: Luther's father and founder of the family business

Edmund Crackenthorpe: Luther's eldest son, killed in the war

Martine Crackenthorpe (unmarried name: Dubois): a French woman, who may have been married to Edmund Crackenthorpe

Anna Stravinska: a French ballet dancer

Armand Dessin: a French police officer in Paris

Madame Joilet: a French woman who manages the Ballet Maritski

Sergeant Wetherall: a Scotland Yard police officer working on the case

Miss Ellis: Harold Crackenthorpe's secretary

Lady Alice Crackenthorpe: Harold's aristocratic wife

Dicky Rogers: a London criminal

Sir Henry Clithering: godfather of Craddock, and friend of Miss Marple

Hillmann: gardener at Rutherford Hall

Sergeant Leakie: a police officer working on the case

Chick Evans: a London criminal

Lady Stoddart-West: James's mother

Sir Robert Stoddart-West: James's father

Dr Morris: the Crackenthorpes' retired doctor

♦ CULTURAL NOTES ♦

1. Paddington Station

This station is situated to the west of the centre of London. It is the main London railway station for trains going to Wales and the West of England, to important cities like Bath, Bristol and Cardiff, and also further south to places like Exeter, Plymouth and Penzance. Agatha Christie lived in the south of Devon, a county in the south west of the UK, so would have been a very frequent traveller to and from Paddington Station whenever she needed to visit London.

All the place names in the story are fictional: Agatha Christie invented them, so they cannot be found on any map.

2. Travel by train in the 1950s

At the time this story was published (1957), the train was the main form of long-distance transport for most people, before cars and motorways changed the way people travelled. There were three classes of travel. The cheapest was third-class, the next was second-class, and the most expensive was first-class, where passengers travelled in much more comfortable railway carriages. This reflected the social classes of the time: working class, middle class and upper class – though British society had already changed a lot after the war, and was about to change dramatically in the 60s.

Tickets were checked by a ticket inspector who walked up and down the train.

Some trains, especially local ones for short distances, had carriages that opened both sides directly onto the platform. Other trains – longer distance ones – had carriages with a corridor running along one side. This enabled people to move from carriage to carriage. This is the case with Mrs McGillicuddy's train at the beginning of the story. However, the train where she saw the murder did not have a corridor. This meant that no one could get into the carriage from another carriage and the murderer could move the body without being seen, if there was no one else in the carriage.

3. Railway architecture
In the story there are several mentions of arches and embankments. When the railways were first built in Britain in the 19th century, they had to be built to avoid steep slopes – rises and falls in the land – as trains had to run along lines that were as flat as possible through the countryside. To make lines run evenly, engineers had to build embankments over low ground. They also had to build bridges over roads, rivers and valleys. These were supported by columns and arches, to take the weight of the train and the line.

4. Life in Britain after World War II
The post-war period in Britain in the 1950s was difficult for most people, as Britain took many years to recover economically from the war. Food was rationed until the middle of the decade (people could only buy a controlled quantity of items like meat, sugar, butter, etc.), and most people had to be very careful with money. This is a constant topic with old Mr Crackenthorpe. Even wealthy people had to make savings and change the often extravagant way they had lived before the war.

Life was also difficult for the many thousands of ex-military men, like Bryan Eastley. They had to find work and adjust to civilian life, after six years of war. Although dangerous, and many thousands of young men died, the war was a time of excitement and opportunity for many. Life afterwards seemed boring and without purpose, especially if they could only get administrative jobs in offices.

5. Boarding schools

Alexander and his friend James go to a boarding school. These are private schools, where the students live during term time, as well as study. They are usually expensive and therefore were at the time of the story (and still are) usually only affordable by wealthy people. Alexander and James are usually hungry and are described as always very interested in the food that Lucy cooks, because food at these boarding schools was often not very good. Although they lived in the school most of the time, they were often allowed to visit their parents at weekends during school terms, and went home during school holidays.

6. Women's Institute

The Women's Institute is a British, community-based organization for women. It was formed in 1915 with two main aims: to develop countryside communities and to encourage women to become more involved in producing food during the First World War.

7. Inquest

When the police investigate a sudden, violent or suspicious death, they often hold a public investigation, called an inquest, to find out why the person died.

At the inquest, a group of people hears medical evidence, as well as evidence from any other people that may be useful. The family of the person who died, and members of the public can also go to the inquest to listen.

If the inquest shows that the death was actually a murder, then the police can arrest and question the suspect. If the police decide that there is enough evidence against the suspect, then this person is officially sent for trial in a court to decide if they are guilty or innocent.

8. Wills and inheritance

A will is a legal document that describes how the money and property that someone leaves when they die is to be distributed to relatives and other people (for example servants or friends). It was very unusual for a person with a fortune not to state where they wanted their money to go. It was therefore of great importance to the children and relatives of a rich person to know the details of their will. Wills were usually made in a solicitor's office but not always. To be legal, the signing of the will has to be witnessed, that is seen, by two people (usually not relatives) who know the person writing the will.

Usually the main part of an inheritance of a wealthy person – their house, land and money – would be inherited by the eldest son if there were several children. In the story, therefore, it is very important for the family to know if Edmund Crackenthorpe was really married and had in fact had a son, as he would inherit the family fortune.

Josiah Crackenthorpe, Luther's father, had left money 'in trust', to be divided amongst his family. 'In trust' means that it is kept separate for a period of time, and invested to provide a regular income. This process is usually managed by lawyers, so that the family members cannot touch the money until the time or circumstances specified in the will.

Luther kept some of his fortune in the form of gold sovereigns – gold coins that are very valuable. He regards them as much safer than paper money.

9. Sotheby's

This is one of the leading international dealers in art and valuable antique furniture, based in the centre of London. It often has sales of paintings and antiques, one of which Harold Crackenthorpe attended in the story.

◆ Glossary ◆

alibi COUNTABLE NOUN
If you have an **alibi**, you can prove that you were somewhere else when a crime was committed

arch COUNTABLE NOUN
An **arch** is a structure that is curved at the top and is supported on either side by a pillar, post, or wall.

arsenic UNCOUNTABLE NOUN
Arsenic is a very strong poison which can kill people.

ballerina COUNTABLE NOUN
A **ballerina** is a woman ballet dancer.

barn COUNTABLE NOUN
A **barn** is a building on a farm in which crops or animal food can be kept.

blind COUNTABLE NOUN
A **blind** is a roll of cloth or paper which you can pull down over a window as a covering.

bohemian ADJECTIVE
You can use **bohemian** to describe artistic people who live in an unconventional way.

boiler COUNTABLE NOUN
A **boiler** is a device which burns gas, oil, electricity, or coal in order to provide hot water, especially for the central heating in a building.

brandy VARIABLE NOUN
Brandy is a strong alcoholic drink which is often drunk after a meal.

caution TRANSITIVE VERB
If the police **caution** someone, they warn them that anything they say may be used as evidence in a trial.

chap COUNTABLE NOUN
Chap is an informal word for a man or boy.

Chief Constable COUNTABLE NOUN
A **Chief Constable** is the officer who is in charge of the police force in a particular county or area in Britain.

choke INTRANSITIVE VERB
When you **choke**, you cannot breathe properly or get enough air into your lungs.

claim COUNTABLE NOUN
A **claim** is something which someone says which they cannot prove and which may be false.

class SUFFIX
First-**class** accommodation is the best and most expensive accommodation on a train or ship. Second-class accommodation on a train or ship is cheaper and less comfortable than first-class.

clock golf UNCOUNTABLE NOUN
Clock golf is type of golf played on a circular area on a lawn.

coach COUNTABLE NOUN
A **coach** is one of the separate sections of a train that carries passengers.

confidential ADJECTIVE
Information that is **confidential** is meant to be kept secret or private.

crowbar COUNTABLE NOUN
A **crowbar** is a heavy iron bar which is used as a lever.

crush TRANSITIVE VERB
To **crush** something means to press it very hard so that its shape is destroyed or so that it breaks into pieces.

dining room COUNTABLE NOUN
The **dining room** is the room in a house where people have their meals, or a room in a hotel where meals are served.

drive COUNTABLE NOUN
A **drive** is a private road leading from a public road to a house.

Dunkirk PROPER NOUN
Dunkirk is a port in France where British and other troops were evacuated from during World War II.

eldest ADJECTIVE
The **eldest** person in a group is the one who was born before all the others.

embankment COUNTABLE NOUN
An **embankment** is a thick wall of earth that is built to carry a road or railway over an area of low ground.

estate COUNTABLE NOUN
Someone's **estate** is all the money and property that they leave behind them when they die.

fingerprint COUNTABLE NOUN
Your **fingerprints** are the marks made by the tip of your fingers when you touch something.

First COUNTABLE NOUN
In British universities, a **First** is an honours degree of the highest standard.

fragile ADJECTIVE
Someone who looks **fragile** looks weak and delicate.

gasp INTRANSITIVE VERB
When you **gasp**, you take a short quick breath through your mouth, especially when you are surprised, shocked, or in pain.

gastro-enteritis UNCOUNTABLE NOUN
Gastro-enteritis is an illness in which the lining of your stomach and intestines becomes swollen and painful.

General COUNTABLE NOUN
A **General** is a senior officer in the armed forces, usually in the army.

give evidence PHRASE
If you **give evidence** in a court of law or an official enquiry, you officially say what you know about people or events, or describe an occasion at which you were present.

godfather COUNTABLE NOUN
If a man is the **godfather** of a younger person, he promises to help bring them up as a Christian.

godson COUNTABLE NOUN
Your **godson** is a person that you promise to help bring up as a Christian.

greenhouse COUNTABLE NOUN
A **greenhouse** is a glass building in which you grow plants that need to be protected from bad weather.

heir COUNTABLE NOUN
An **heir** is someone who has the right to inherit a person's money, property, or title when that person dies.

housing estate COUNTABLE NOUN
A **housing estate** is a large number of houses or flats built close together at the same time.

in ruins PHRASE
If a building or place is **in ruins**, most of it has been destroyed and only parts of it remain.

in trust PHRASE
If something valuable is kept in trust, it is held and protected by a group of people or an organization on behalf of other people.

inherit TRANSITIVE VERB
If you **inherit** money or property, you receive it from someone who has died.

innocent COUNTABLE NOUN
An **innocent** is someone who has no experience or knowledge of the more complex or unpleasant aspects of life.

inquest COUNTABLE NOUN
When an **inquest** is held, a public official hears evidence about someone's death in order to find out the cause.

invalid COUNTABLE NOUN
An **invalid** is someone who needs to be cared for because they have an illness or disability.

ladyship COUNTABLE NOUN
In Britain, you use the expression her **ladyship** when you are addressing or referring to female members of the nobility or the wives of knights.

large-scale ADJECTIVE
A **large-scale** map or diagram represents a small area of land or a building or machine on a scale that is large enough for small details to be shown.

lawn COUNTABLE NOUN
A **lawn** is an area of grass that is kept cut short and is usually part of someone's garden or backyard, or part of a park.

-like SUFFIX
-like combines with some nouns to form adjectives which describe something or someone as being similar to the noun. For example, if someone is business-like, you mean that they deal with things in an efficient way, as if they were running a business.

lord TITLE NOUN
In Britain, a **lord** is a man who has a high rank in the nobility, for example an earl, a viscount, or a marquis.

manservant COUNTABLE NOUN
A **manservant** is a man who works as a servant in a private house.

master COUNTABLE NOUN
A **master** of a household is the head of the household.

occupy TRANSITIVE VERB
If you are **occupied** with something, you are busy doing that thing or thinking about it.
TRANSITIVE VERB
If a group of people or an army **occupies** a place or country, they move into it, using force in order to gain control of it.

parallel ADJECTIVE
If two objects are **parallel**, they are the same distance apart along their whole length.

pastry UNCOUNTABLE NOUN
Pastry is a food made from flour, fat, and water that is mixed together, rolled flat, and baked in the oven. It is used, for example, for making pies.

pigsty COUNTABLE NOUN
A **pigsty** is an enclosed place where pigs are kept on a farm.

plain ADJECTIVE
If you describe someone, especially a woman or girl, as **plain**, you think they look ordinary and are not at all beautiful.

poisoner COUNTABLE NOUN
A **poisoner** is someone who has killed or harmed another person by using poison.

porter COUNTABLE NOUN
A **porter** is a person whose job is to carry things, for example people's luggage at a railway station or in a hotel.

powder compact COUNTABLE NOUN
A **powder compact** is a small flat case which contains a mirror and face powder and is often carried in a woman's handbag.

refrigerator COUNTABLE NOUN
A **refrigerator** is a large container which is kept cool inside, usually by electricity, so that the food and drink in it stays fresh.

sarcophagus COUNTABLE NOUN
A **sarcophagus** is a large decorative container in which a dead body was placed in ancient times.

scholar COUNTABLE NOUN
A **scholar** is a person who studies an academic subject and knows a lot about it.

Scotland Yard PROPER NOUN
Scotland Yard is the headquarters of the police force in London.

sip COUNTABLE NOUN
A **sip** is a small amount of drink that you take into your mouth.

softened INTRANSITIVE VERB
If your face or expression **softens**, it becomes much more gentle and friendly.

Soho PROPER NOUN
Soho is a district in central London, known for its restaurants and nightclubs.

Sotheby's PROPER NOUN
Sotheby's is a famous auction house which specializes in jewellery, antiques, and fine art.

sovereign COUNTABLE NOUN
A **sovereign** is a gold coin which was used in Britain in the past.

spirited ADJECTIVE
A **spirited** person is very active, lively, and confident.

Squadron Leader COUNTABLE NOUN
A **Squadron Leader** is an officer
of middle rank in the British air
force.

strangle TRANSITIVE VERB
To **strangle** someone means to
kill them by tightly squeezing
their throat.

swear INTRANSITIVE VERB
If you say that you can **swear** to
something being true, you are
saying very firmly that it is true.

telegram COUNTABLE NOUN
A **telegram** is a message that is
sent by telegraph and then
printed and delivered to
someone's home or office.

terms PLURAL NOUN
The **terms** of an agreement,
treaty, or other arrangement are
the conditions that must be
accepted by the people involved
in it.

thank goodness PHRASE
You say '**thank goodness**' when
you are very relieved about
something.

theatrical company COUNTABLE
NOUN
A **theatrical company** is an
organization that produces
performances for the theatre.

track COUNTABLE NOUN
Railway **tracks** are the rails that a
train travels along.

uncomfortably ADVERB
If do something **uncomfortably**,
you do it in a way that shows you
are slightly worried or
embarrassed, and not relaxed and
confident.

unwillingly ADVERB
If you do something **unwillingly**,
you do not want to do it and will
not agree to do it.

vicar COUNTABLE NOUN
A **vicar** is an Anglican priest who
is in charge of a church and the
area it is in, which is called a parish.

weed COUNTABLE NOUN
A **weed** is a wild plant that grows
in gardens or fields of crops and
prevents the plants that you want
from growing properly.

will COUNTABLE NOUN
A **will** is a legal document saying what you want to happen to your money and property when you die.

Yorkshire pudding VARIABLE NOUN
Yorkshire pudding is a British food which is made by baking a thick liquid mixture of flour, milk, and eggs. It is often eaten with roast beef.

Your home is your castle PHRASE
The expression '**Your home is your castle**' is used to say that people should be able to do what they want in their own homes and not be told what to do there.

COLLINS ENGLISH READERS ONLINE

Go online to discover the following useful resources for teachers and students:

- Downloadable audio of the story

- Classroom activities, including a plot synopsis

- Student activities, suitable for class use or for self-studying learners

- A level checker to ensure you are reading at the correct level

- Information on the Collins COBUILD Grading Scheme

All this and more at **www.collinselt.com/readers**